TWELVE

Have fun diving into
Marley's world! :)

TWELVE

M. L. Williams

gatekeeper press™

Columbus, Ohio

This book is a work of fiction. The names, characters and events in this book are the products of the author's imagination or are used fictitiously. Any similarity to real persons living or dead is coincidental and not intended by the author.

Twelve

Published by Gatekeeper Press
2167 Stringtown Rd, Suite 109
Columbus, OH 43123-2989
www.GatekeeperPress.com

The editorial work for this book is entirely the product of the author. Gatekeeper Press did not participate in and is not responsible for any aspect of this element.

Library of Congress Control Number: 2020951330

Special thanks to Carol Thompson, for editing my book. She is an editor and proofreader for Reader's Favorites. And Tamara Beach proofread and edited my book. She has been editing books for six years, both for indie authors and for a small publishing company.

ISBN (hardcover): 9781662907944
ISBN (paperback): 9781662907951
eISBN: 9781662907968

Contents

Chapter 1

You ever keep a secret so big you're dying to let it out? I'm going on a Guinness World Record here keeping a twelve-year-long secret that only I know. That's right, I haven't told a soul. I'm not dying to let the world know what the secret is exactly; I'd prefer that the world doesn't know. I'm just tired of holding it in. So this is my way to release it. This story may or may not be your typical "happily ever after" hurrah that people drool over but, it will be a story. We can find out what the "ever after" is together, but to get to that, we'll have to rewind twelve years to when I was in the seventh grade at Pellman Junior High.

You see, when you're someone like me, you have to be careful. What you do and what you say can and will be used against you in the court of law. Just kidding; not in this case, but let me tell you, middle schoolers love gossiping as much as adults love taking naps.

I didn't figure out who I truly was until my second year of high school, and that's what makes my junior high experience that much more special...

I'm a five-foot-six-inch caramel-toned black girl with pigtails. I'm sure this is hard to imagine, but that was me in the seventh grade. Picture Darla from *Finding Nemo*, make her light-skinned, give her dark-brown eyes and hair, remove the braces (add them back next year), and there you have me. Cute, right?

It was the only first day of school I will never forget: the first day of seventh grade.

I remember walking into school with my schedule in hand, nervous because I didn't know if I would have my friends in my classes. This was a big deal; you would pretty much just drop dead on the spot if your friends weren't in your class. Pretty dramatic, to say the least, but it was an unanimous decision made by all junior high students in America.

My first class of the day was English with Mr. Turner. How cliché, when is English not the first class of the day...

ᔐ

"Okay, class," says Mr. Turner. "We are going to start the day with a fun exercise so we can get to know each other."

Of course, we are. Oh, and by the way, my friends are *not* in this class, so please understand my wholehearted excitement to do this exercise.

"Grab a partner," he says, shutting the classroom door.

Yes, music to my ears, especially with my archenemies in this class. Wait, I haven't explained this—

"And stand next to them back-to-back," he continues.

Okay, so now everyone is grabbing a partner. I failed to mention that our grades are split into two "teams" at this school, just a fancy way of splitting our grade in half since we have so many students. Last year, there was 601 and 602; I was on 601, the best team you could possibly be on. Naturally, we became a family and 602 became our archenemy. This year, I'm on 701, and I kid you not, it feels like the entire 602 has invaded 701, so I'm in what feels like prison. I can only think, "How could they let these peasants invade our territory?" By the way, if you didn't already know, I'm very dramatic and I'm pretty sure the teams are chosen at complete random.

Anyway, class finally ends after what feels like an eternity. How do fifty-minute classes feel like six years? How is that possible? I thought I'd rot in class with how excruciatingly long they are.

The bell rings, thank god. Everyone grabs their things and runs out as if the room just burst into flames. We have a five-minute passing time that feels like fifteen seconds compared to the eternity of class. All the while, you have teachers yelling at you to "*Get to class!*" as soon as your pinky toe steps out of the previous class.

"Yo, Marley!" I hear as I'm trying my locker combination for the twentieth time. I turn to see that it's my best friend, Teagan. I can smile and breathe again.

"Teagan!" I yell. "Dude, let me see your schedule *right now.*" I begin comparing, and I realize the heavens must have seen my disparity because Teagan and I have every class together except for first-hour English and our electives. I can live with that. We celebrate for a mere three seconds before we are told to get to class. We happily oblige.

For those who don't know, electives are your fun classes. Like P.E., home ed, art, and all the good stuff that we truly go to school for. This is a joke, kind of.

Lunchtime came around, and I finally get to see more of my friends. Teagan and I are the first to find a place to sit.

I met Teagan last year in my science class. Meeting her was different. She was new to Pellman so she didn't know anyone coming from Pellman Elementary like a lot of our classmates did. I would catch her staring at me in class, and after a few days, I finally decided to ask her why in the hell she kept staring at me. She told me she thought we should be friends. Talk about the beginning of a serial killer novel. Now that I think about it, being eleven, that sounds like a pretty normal start to a sixth-grade friendship, but eleven-year-old me had my eye on her in case she decided to throw me into the janitor's closet and suffocate me one day. I watched *a lot* of Disney Channel, which doesn't exactly correlate, but you get my dramatic fiction.

"Hey, uglies!"

We turn to see Dakota running up to our table. I have mixed feelings about Dakota. We've been archenemies on the basketball court with our summer teams, and this is the first year we will actually become teammates. Joy.

"Hey, Dakota," I say. "Ready for basketball this year?"

"Of course, I'm ready. I stay ready! I'm going to be captain," she says with a Cruella de Vil smirk.

"Great," I'm thinking.

Teagan chimes in. "I'm so excited to play with you guys; we are going to be so good."

Dakota replies, "Teagan, do you even know how to dribble a basketball?!"

"Yes, I do, Dakota," says Teagan.

"We will see," says Dakota as she laughs uncontrollably loud.

I sit in silence; I usually don't talk much when I don't feel comfortable. I didn't know Dakota all that well other than when our AAU teams would go head to head what felt like every other tournament.

We spend the rest of lunch talking about our summers and the upcoming basketball tryouts. A few more friends sneak over as lunch goes on. Yes, they sneak because, you see, when you find a place to sit in the cafeteria, you cannot, by any means, move to a new table or you'll be detained on the spot. Slightly dramatic, but our lunch monitors are like S.W.A.T.

Lunch is over, and it's finally time for the best part of the day: electives.

My first elective is art. I walk in to find that the seating isn't the classic row-by-row seating chart. There are only chairs aligned on the walls of the room. Weird. The chairs fill in with classmates and class begins.

"Hiya, folks. I'm Mr. Blake, and this is art. If this class isn't on your schedule, let's have a look so I can get you where you need to be."

I look down just to double-check, and it turns out I'm not too shabby of a reader because I'm in the right class. Okay, so far so good.

"Okay, let's do a roll call so I can give you a quick background of what we will be doing this semester. After I call your name, tell us one thing we should know about you," announces Mr. Blake.

Oh god, now I have to actually talk. Have mercy on me.

Mr. Blake begins roll call, and I begin overanalyzing how I will say my "here." Or should I say "present?" *Shit, I should probably clear my throat.*

I try to clear my throat without sounding like I'm clearing my throat just to say, "Here."

All bad. Overthinking how in the hell to say "here." Have I already hit rock bottom on the first day of school? I hate talking in front of people; I get nervous when all eyes are on me.

Not paying attention, because, well, I'm hyperventilating inside my head on how to say "here," my classmate taps me on my shoulder.

"Marley," Laura says, grunting at me.

I look up, confused. "Yeah?"

She's giving me the look, so I look up at Mr. Blake. He's apparently called out my name twice so far. Kill me now. If all eyes weren't on me before, they are now.

"Are you Marley Waters?" says Mr. Blake.

"Yeah," I say as I feel my body overheating.

"Perfect. What's something you want the class to know about you?" he asks.

I reach for my go-to in times of emergency. "I-I play basketball," I stutter.

"That's awesome; do you plan on playing on this year's team?"

I'm thinking, "No, no, no, please stop talking to me."

Dying inside, I respond, "Yes, I do. I'm excited."

"Great, I can't wait to see you play," he says, marking on his notebook. I'm assuming he was checking that I'm present in class.

"Thanks," I say as I look back down at my pencil.

Mr. Blake finishes roll call and begins explaining what we will be doing and learning throughout the course of the semester. I hear something about woodburning, which sounds pretty awesome; for the rest of his spiel, I was daydreaming.

I have a reputation for being an awesome basketball player and super athletic, which got annoying as I got older because I wanted to be seen as more than just a basketball player. Being in art made me feel different, as did being enrolled in advanced math.

The bell rings, and this time I'm upset because *now* time chooses to fly by. Yeah, I was embarrassed earlier, but I enjoyed the sense of freedom in here. So, I tell myself, "until tomorrow" and get my things together.

I begin walking toward the door, and in that moment, a classmate drops her binder. Her papers fly everywhere. A few kids laugh and keep walking. I look at them and shake my head, and go over to her to help her gather her things. I kneel and start grabbing papers.

"Oh, thanks," she says.

"No problem, it happens to the best of us," I reply.

We don't say much else until we grab them all and align them back through the rings.

"All right, last one," I say as I close the rings.

She stands. "Thank you again," she says.

I grab my binder and push myself off the floor. Before I can say, "You're welcome," I look at her for the first time and my entire body goes numb.

She has tan skin and short brown hair. But I am absolutely mesmerized by her honey-glazed brown eyes. She's staring straight at me.

I'm speechless.

She smirks and says she'll see me tomorrow.

I spend the rest of the day thinking about that encounter. Who is she? Something about that felt different...

"Today actually wasn't too bad. This year might be the best year yet," Teagan says as we walk to our lockers after our last class.

I can't stop thinking about art, so I don't hear her.

"Mar?" Teagan says.

I snap back to life. "Yeah? Sorry, my bad," I respond.

"Are you good?" she says.

"Yeah, sorry, just thinking about all of this work we're going to have for math," I make up on the spot.

Teagan laughs. "Don't worry about any of that, we'll take it one day at a time."

I'm not worried about math at all. I love math, and I excel exponentially in the subject. Teagan knows this, but I had to make something up, right? What could I have said? "Oh, I ran into this girl in my class and I thought she was heaven on earth." Yeah, no. Absolutely not. Plus, I'm not into girls. I'm into guys.

We pack up our things and go downstairs to the bus lines. For some reason, I find myself searching—looking over every person as we walk to the lines.

"Bus seventy-one," calls the bus monitor.

"That's my cue," I tell Teagan. "See ya tomorrow. I'll talk to you on MySpace!"

You see, it's 2008, and texting is a thing, but like not a thing. Most of us can text, but there are limits or they cost extra per text, so we use MySpace.

"Okay, bye, Mar!" replies Teagan.

On the bus ride home, I can't stop thinking about the girl I ran into. I mean, wow...I've never been so starstruck like this. I can't wait to see her again.

Chapter 2

A few days go by and pretty much everyone has settled into school. First-hour English is still as dreadful as the first day of school. My other classes are cool; I have Teagan in most of them, so we usually laugh and pass notes the whole time.

My classmates are different than most classmates from other schools. We're all friends. We don't have statuses or the "popular kids" or anything of the sort. We're all just cool. We don't care who has money or who doesn't. It's pretty much a parallel universe, and it's awesome. Oh, yeah, I kind of got over the fact that 602 invaded my team. Turned out they weren't too shabby...

I can't breathe in art class anymore. The girl I ran into on the first day literally takes my breath away. We're on our sixth day of school, and I haven't said anything to her since I helped her on the first day. I haven't even been able to look at her. I still don't even know her name.

Little do I know that will change today.

"Class, I'm going put you into groups of four, and I want you to create a city out of these Legos," Mr. Blake says as he's gathering a shit ton of Legos in plastic containers.

The best part of this is that I don't have to frantically choose my groupmates.

"Group one will be Freddy, Xavier, Madison, and Chelsie."

"Group two will be Laura, Marley, Brandon, and Jess."

I gather my things to meet my groupmates as he called out the rest of the groups. We all navigate to Laura. I have no idea why.

"Hey, Marley," Laura greets.

"Hey," I reply and sit.

Brandon slams his body down on the ground because that's what seventh-grade boys do.

"What's crackin', ladies?!" he says.

"Was that necessary? I mean, I'm assuming so," I say to him in my dry humor.

Laura laughs and responds, "Gosh, Brandon. You are so crazy. Wait, where is Jess?"

I look up at Laura, confused. "Who's Jess?" I ask.

She ignores me and squeals, "Oh, here she comes! Yay, we're all here!"

Little did I know my heart was about to stop in less than two seconds.

Jess sits down and gives the group a smirk with a wave. It's the binder girl, and I can't look.

Mr. Blake drops off our Legos and tells us we have thirty minutes to create a city. We get started.

"Okay, I'll take point with building the skyscrapers. Brandon, you build—"

"What I want," he says abruptly.

I glance at Brandon. *Uh, okay...*

Jess and I make that "awkward-situation" face at each other and smirk. We can tell they will be fun.

"How about we just start building and see what happens?" I say, ignoring Laura and Brandon's bicker.

"Fine," Laura responds.

"Great," I say, grabbing my first Lego.

Laura starts up small chatter. "So, Jess, are you on 701 or 702?" she asks.

I'm trying so hard not to be overly interested because I'm dying to know this answer. I continue connecting Legos.

"I'm 702," she replies.

Dammit.

"Aw, that's too bad. At least we have this class together!" Laura says.

Jess smiles and continues working.

I glance at her and realize she might be shyer than me. That's a new one.

"You play any sports?" Brandon asks Jess.

"Yeah, I play tennis," she says, glancing at him and looking back down at her Legos. "What about you?"

"I play football and basketball," he replies.

"Nice," she says.

We keep working. I kid you not, the oxygen in my body feels nonexistent. Focusing on my work and the fact that Jess has been in my circumference for twenty-three minutes has been overwhelming. Luckily, I'm a professional at keeping it cool…I think.

"Okay, let's see what we have here," Mr. Blake says as he walks up to our group.

"Laura, take it away," I say in a not-so-sarcastic but sarcastic voice. Laura seems like she'd do well in the leadership position of our group. I sure as hell aren't taking the job.

"Yes! Okay, so…"

Laura goes on to tell Mr. Blake some random story. I'm pretty sure we built a classic downtown city, but apparently, that turned into a modern, technological city that gets its power from flashlight batteries or whatever the hell she made up. She definitely went off-script; we probably shouldn't have given her that authority.

Mr. Blake is oddly impressed and gives us an A.

Well, okay then. I'll take it, but I don't know what just happened.

Hmm, I kind of like these kids. Different, but I like them. Laura's a handful, but she's all right in my book.

We begin packing up our things when Mr. Blake makes one last announcement. "Class, these will be the groups you sit in every day for the remainder of the semester. Get to know one another."

I think I just fainted. Not sure yet.

"Oh, my gosh, yes! I love this group!" Laura squeals.

"This will be fun," Brandon adds.

"We'll see," I slip in.

Jess doesn't say anything, but I can tell she's happy about it. She has this small, faint but cute smile on her face. Well, not cute, but like a nice smile. You get what I mean.

"Wait. Let's exchange numbers," Laura says before I can sprint out of the room.

I look at her. "Huh?"

"Let's exchange numbers! We can group text each other," she replies.

"Okay, fine," Brandon says as he rips off three pieces of paper and writes down his number.

I think I'm going to have a heart attack.

I take out a piece of paper and write my number three times, my hand is shaking. I hand them to everyone without shitting my pants, especially when I hand one to Jess. I make eye contact with her for a half-second.

Jess hands her papers to Brandon and Laura, and I feel like they turned into roadrunners and sprinted out of the room, leaving us in the room by ourselves.

"Here you go," she says, handing me the paper.

"Thanks," I say, playing it cool.

She smiles and starts walking away. I grab my binder off the floor and I hear, "I'll text you after school."

I freeze and look up. Jess is standing in the doorway.

"I thought we're supposed to group text?" I respond, still playing it cool with a confused look.

"I know." She smirks and walks out.

Marley, breathe.

Oh my god, did that just happen?

"Stop. We're cool. It's not like that. I'm not like that," I whisper to myself.

I can't even tell you what the rest of the day was like. I just wanted school to be over. Teagan blabbed on and on about homework and classes all day, and Dakota was being Dakota. My game of "Where's Jess?" came to an end since I found out she's on 702. Bummer.

The bell rings, and I powerwalk to my locker so I can look at my phone. My heart starts pounding. I wish I could relax. She's not going to text me in this very moment. She may not even text me at all.

I get home and start on my homework. I can't have my phone out until it's complete, so my mom hides it. Whack, I know. But I don't blame her. I can get distracted, especially on a day like this one.

I finish my homework. I go to show Mom so I can get my phone back. She makes a few comments about my handwriting, but that's nothing new. I pretend to be sorry about it and grab my phone. The first thing I do is check my messages. I have a few from a group text with Teagan and Dakota, but nothing spectacular. What I mean is I don't have a message from Jess, so I head outside to play basketball with my friends.

After an hour, I come inside and shower so I can be ready for dinner. Still no text. *Ugh.*

"Stop obsessing over this text message, Marley," I say to myself.

I head to the kitchen to start chowing down my dinner.

"How was school?" my mom asks my sister Kendal and me.

"Good. We got to play with Legos so that was fun," I reply as I sit down.

"It was fine. We have basketball tryouts coming up soon," my sister chimes in.

"Oh, crap, so do we," I add.

"I don't know if I want to play this year. I think I only want to focus on track," she says, looking nervously at Mom.

Kendal is a sophomore in high school, by the way.

"Ken, I want you to do what you love. If that's only track, then so be it," Mom says, tasting the lemonade.

Kendal smiles from ear to ear. I know track is her passion. I think she only played basketball because both of our parents did. She probably didn't want to disappoint them. I'm glad Mom is accepting her choice. My dad might not have the same reaction.

Dad doesn't live with us; my parents are divorced. Spare me the pity. I'm fine. I'm not damaged from it. Hey, I get two Christmases, two birthdays, two of everything. Plus, my parents are still friends; they just didn't work out. Mom says that happens in life sometimes.

"Mar, figure out your practice time so I can get carpool-situated," Mom say as she fixes her plate.

"Okey-doke," I say. We start eating.

Dinner is pretty good, if I must say so myself. We're having my favorite—taco salad.

I finish and go to my room to watch TV before bed. As I toss my phone onto my pillow, it buzzes.

Jess (9:42 p.m.): hi

HOLY CRAP. Okay. Play it cool, Marley. Do the ol' take-five-minutes-to-respond-so-you-don't-seem-crazy trick.

I wait five minutes to respond, watching the clock move like it does in English.

Okay, here I go.

Me (9:47 p.m.): hey

Oh god, was that too plain? Why am I acting like this?

Jess (9:49 p.m.): I told you I would text you

Me (9:50 p.m.): I didn't believe you

Dear god, Marley, what are you saying right now. Stop texting so fast.

Jess (9:50 p.m.): why?

Me (9:55 p.m.): I don't know. We don't really talk.

Jess (9:59 p.m.): haha we just met

Me (10:04 p.m.): very true

I don't know if saying less is the playing-it-cool move, or if I'm completely blowing this. She's going to think I'm so weird.

Jess (10:08 p.m.): haha so we have to get to know each other

My phone buzzes again; it's Laura. I ignore it and text Jess back.

Me (10:10 p.m.): did you want to do the group text?

Jess (10:16 p.m.): Not really

Me (10:16 p.m.): Oh okay.

Jess (10:17 p.m.): Did you?

Me (10:19 p.m.): Well, no not really. Haha.

Jess (10:22 p.m.): hahah okay then, no group text

Me (10:24 p.m.): cool.

Jess (10:27 p.m.): what are you doing?

Me (10:27 p.m.): besides watching tv, nothing really.

Jess (10:28 p.m.): me too

Me (10:33 p.m.): what are you watching?

Jess (10:41 p.m.): Hannah Montana

Me (10:46 p.m.): omg me too, haha.

Jess (10:52 p.m.): Hahahah, I love this show

Me (10:59 p.m.): so do I lol.

Jess (11:07 p.m.): who's your favorite character?

Me (11:09 p.m.): Jackson for sure. I love Miley though.

Jess (11:14 p.m.): haha I love Lily

I feel like I should end the conversation. I think I can talk to her all night.

Me (11:21 p.m.): Nice, lol. I should probably go to sleep. I hate getting up in the mornings.

Jess (11:23 p.m.): me too. see you tomorrow. night. Oh and thanks again for the other day.

Me (11:24 p.m.): you're welcome. Night.

As I set my alarm and put my phone under my pillow, I realize I didn't text any of my friends back, including the group text that Laura started. I meant to at least say hi. Oops. Tomorrow might be awkward, but I don't care. Something is different about Jess, she's cooler than cool as lame as that sounds.

⤳

I feel butterflies in my stomach as I walk into art class. Jess is here already at our table. I must act cool.

I stop to chat with Ben Bohanan. He's one hundred percent geek and really nice. I ask him how his science fair project is coming along. He starts to talk, but I'm not listening. I'm thinking about Jess. I hope she doesn't look at me.

I'm so rude. Using Ben as a decoy, or something like that. He stops talking and I tell him that I can't wait to see his project and dart for my seat, hoping he didn't notice my disinterest.

"Hi," I say as I sit. "I wonder what we'll be doing today."

"Something fun, I hope," Jess says. I nod and smile. I can't turn my head to look at her. I think I'd stare or do something stupid, like drool.

God help me. I'm out of control.

Just as I turn to talk to Laura, a pack of Juicy Fruit gum floats in front of me. I turn.

"Gum?" Jess asks.

"Oh, sure," I say and start to take a stick.

"No, no," she says. "Take the whole pack. I have more. Do you guys want one?" she asks the others.

They are quick to grab them.

I'm never going to chew this gum. I'm going to cherish it forever. I place it in my hoodie pouch.

Did I mention how much I love this hoodie? My grandma got it for me for Christmas last year. She made it herself. She knitted it with yarn that she let me pick out and she stitched my basketball number on the front. It's blue and gold, just like our school colors. There's no way anyone could ever tell that it's handmade. She's that good with the knitting needles.

Now, my favorite hoodie is holding the pack of gum from my new favorite person. Wait, did I just say that?

We work on abstract painting and it's a lot of fun. We get to talk and laugh. That's what I like about art. It's not all boring like regular classes, and, well, if you haven't figured it out…Jess is here.

The bell rings. I hate when art ends. But the day must go on. I say goodbye to Jess and thank her for the gum.

I head for my next class, and Teagan flags me down. We walk together.

"Hey, Mar," she starts, "Have you seen that new boy Sam?"

"Um, no."

"He's fiiiine," she says in her exaggerated voice. "I've got to get to know him."

"You're boy crazy," I say, shaking my head. "You said the same thing about Cameron at orientation!"

"Well, you aren't just yet. You never talk about boys. In the year I've known you, I don't think you've talked about any boy."

Oh, boy. The boys complaint. Here we go.

"I like to put all of my energy into basketball. You know, my mom says if I keep it up through high school, I can get a sports scholarship to college," I say.

Good save, Marley. I'm rather proud of myself for that one.

"Oh, yeah. I see," says Teagan. "That makes sense. Boys can screw things up, at least that's what my mom's always telling me."

"They can. I mean, think about it, T. You like a boy and a boy likes you and you're in the same class. You look at him and he looks at you, and you have no clue what the teacher is saying. It's how it always goes. *Major* distraction."

Ooo, Mar. Sounding very adult-like. Thanks, Mom.

We walk into our classroom, and I am relieved that conversation is over. I don't like explaining myself. I mean, I like boys and all, but there aren't any in this school that make me do a double-take. I'm really fine and content.

The day goes by slowly, and finally, the last class of the day arrives. I can't wait to get home and turn on my phone to see if Jess sent me a message.

Miss Smith, our science teacher, talks about plant life. I really don't care about it. I just want to go home.

The bell finally rings. I throw my books in my locker and head for the main door. Mom is picking me up today. I have an appointment with the orthodontist. I know. Be jealous.

I jump into Mom's car and toss the pack of gum on the console. The last thing I need is a lecture from the orthodontist about chewing gum, sugar causing tooth decay, and then there's Mom's perpetual worry that I'll choke… because at times she still thinks I'm three.

In her defense, I did get a hold of a pack of gum that Kendal had, loaded a few sticks in my mouth, and somehow managed to lodge the wad in my throat. I won't get into the gory details; I'll just say it wasn't pretty.

After a long wait and a short exam, we get in the car and head home. I have to get spacers before I can get braces. Great.

"I swear I had some change in the ashtray," Mom says, perplexed. "I was going to use it to have you run in the store and grab a tomato for the salad I'm making for dinner," she says. "I wasn't going to break a bill if I didn't have to. Oh, well. I must have used it for the last tomato."

I turn on my phone and tune out Mom. Her quarters are missing. What can I say? She's getting on in years, so she's probably getting forgetful. What is she now…thirty-five? Yeah, she's close to needing a nursing home.

I don't have any messages.

Bummer.

I decide I'd better put my gum in my pocket before I forget. But…

Where did it go? I know I put it right here. Or was it there? Um…

"Mom, did you take my pack of Juicy Fruit?" I ask.

"No, I didn't. And why do you have gum? Not with the money I'm about to spend on your teeth."

"A friend gave it to me. I wasn't going to chew it, but I want to keep it."

She looks at me like she's Sherlock Holmes. "What friend? Some boy?"

"No, Mom. Just a new friend I met. This is like the friendship offering, you know, like the silly things you did back in your day."

"Well, that was nice of them," she says, ignoring my back-in-her-day remark. She does that sometimes. Ignorance is bliss, I guess.

We pull in our driveway and I search everywhere for my gum. Nothing. It didn't just get up and walk away, as Mom would say.

I check under the seats and between the seats. Still nothing.

I'm not sure how it could have disappeared like that.

I walk into the house and Mom is listening to a message on our answering machine. She turns to me.

"Are you missing anything else from the car?" she whispers.

I'm not sure why she's whispering, so I shake my head.

"Well," she says when she's finished listening to the message, "that was the orthodontist's office. Apparently, someone riffled through the cars in the parking lot this afternoon. Whoever it was got my change. The receptionist said a few unlocked cars were robbed."

My heart sinks to my knees. Suddenly, I realize my pack of gum is probably getting chewed at this very moment by some ex-con covered in tattoos with no teeth or maybe braces.

Mom never locks the car. Maybe now she will.

Goodbye, gum. I hope this isn't an omen.

⌒

Dinner was good, sans tomato. Luckily, I'm not the biggest fan of them.

I eat and head to my bedroom, anxious to get my homework finished so I can have my phone.

I am pleased with the speed I finish, and I march downstairs to show Mom. She hands me my phone.

I have a message, and it's from Jess! Maybe I'm a little too excited.

Jess (6:15 p.m.): Hey, enjoying the gum? :)

Crap. You weren't supposed to speak of the gum ever again, Jess.

Me (6:17 p.m.): I'm saving it

I lied. I had to lie. How do I tell her I left it in my mom's car while I was at the orthodontist and some thug stole it along with our tomato money?

Jess (6:18 p.m.): Chewed or unchewed

Me (6:19 p.m.): very funny

Jess (6:22 p.m.): Did you see the new kid Sam? He rides my bus. He's really cute :)

Me (6:24 p.m.): Haven't seen him but I've been told he's hot

Jess (6:25 p.m.): Sure is!

Well, I guess she's going to be in competition with Teagan for Sam. She likes boys. I mean, that's not surprising. Isn't that what twelve-year-old girls are supposed to do?

Me (6:29 p.m.): Good luck. I hope you get to be Mrs. Sam soon! Haha

Another lie. This isn't the best way to begin a friendship. She messages me back with a "thank you," and that's the end of the chat.

I hear screaming coming from downstairs, and I run down as fast as my legs will carry me. It's Kendal. She's having a meltdown. It seems her reading glasses are missing from the car. This is one heck of a thug. Now he can see better when he opens *my* gum and when he spends the tomato money. I hope he's happy that we had a tomato-deprived salad for dinner. Well, maybe it's a she, but I guess the receptionist did say one of the patients saw a man running from the parking lot.

The gum thief. I think it will be title of my next essay for English class.

Chapter 3

It's the first basketball game of the season; the school threw an assembly for us, so it included the *entire* seventh grade.

"Okay, girls and boys, everyone is in the gym already, so we're about to go in," Coach Leslie says.

Dakota is already loving the attention.

"We rep the Sharks, Sharks, Sharks!" she sings as everyone chimes in.

We run into the gym and rip the banner that was custom made for us, and the entire seventh grade is roaring. It feels like a movie. I won't lie, it's pretty cool.

Principal Miller calms the crowd.

"Ladies and gentlemen, boys and girls, your 2008 Sharks basketball teams!"

Everyone goes crazy, screaming uncontrollably and stomping their feet on the bleachers.

I smile as I find myself surfing the crowd for one particular person.

Nothing.

"We're going to let our captains say a few words," Principal Miller says loudly into the mic.

I look up from crowd surfing. "Uhh, what?" I say to Dakota.

"Yeah, we get to say something about the game tonight!" she says, overly excited.

Great, just great. I was fine with the display, but the speaking is where you lose me.

"Okay, you can just speak for us both," I say hesitantly.

"No, Marley, they wanna hear from us both!" Dakota says with the big smile on her face.

"Okay, fine," I say.

What am I going to say? I couldn't even say "here" in front of a class of fifteen students and now I have to talk in front of three hundred. Best day ever.

Principal Miller starts out with the boys' captain, who happens to be my good friend Brandon from art. While he's talking, my eyes are back into the crowd.

After searching high and low, I find a group of familiar friends and lo and behold, there she is. Jess is sitting in the far-right corner of the gym but on the front row of the bleachers. She sees me looking in her direction, so she smiles softly with a small wave. I smile back and start to wave until I am pulled abruptly on my shoulder by Dakota.

"What the hell?" I say angrily.

"It's your turn, dummy."

"Oh. Crap," I say as I grab the mic.

"Marley!" someone calls out from the stands. That leads to three other people doing the same. I take one-seventh of a second to glance at Jess, and she's laughing at them. I smile softly and begin my spiel.

"Hey...um, hope to see you guys tonight," is all my body let me say. I hand the mic back to Principal Miller.

"That was it?" Dakota teases.

"I'm not good at speaking in public like that," I reply.

Teagan chimes in, "You did good, Marley. Dakota, stop teasing."

"Whatever," she replies.

Before we exit the gym, Principal Miller has us line up in front of the doors to high-five students as they leave. We cheer to our classmates as they come through. It's really fun seeing all of my 601 friends. I miss them. There are so many people I can't pay attention to when Jess is getting close. I'll probably miss her. As I talk to Teagan, instead of giving me a high five, someone gives me a light push. I turn around and before I can react, Jess is walking past me giving her high fives to the rest of the team. I smile softly and hand out the remaining high fives.

After it's over, I take off for the locker room to grab my things.

"Marley!" I hear Dakota yelling as we're walking to the locker room.

"What's up?" I reply.

"I have something juicy," she says in a real mischievous way.

"Okay, and what's that?" I frown.

"Don't tell him I told you, but David likes you," she says, smiling awkwardly big.

"Oh, wow. Um, I—"

"Hey, Marley!"

I turn around to see David behind me. "Hey, David," I respond.

Dakota stands there looking like the Kool-Aid man while Teagan looks like she's watching a tornado pass by.

"I wanted to tell you that I like you and think we should date."

Yes, this is how all junior high relationships begin. Never talked before, just do it. Woo.

"Do it!" Dakota yells.

"Okay," I say.

Dakota and Teagan dance as if I was just married. David and I smile awkwardly and go into our respective locker rooms.

I won't hear the end of this one.

"Oh my gosh. You guys, Marley and David are dating!" Dakota yells to our teammates.

Let my nightmare begin.

So, yeah, David is cool. He's attractive. Do I know why I'm dating him? Not really, other than the fact that I think I'm supposed to because, you know, I'm a girl and he's a guy. So, yeah, man, let's do this.

I don't see Jess the rest of the day, and we had art before the assembly, so I won't get to tell her until school's over. I'm just hoping word doesn't get out too fast, but with Dakota around with a bullhorn for a mouth, I don't have high hopes...

As I'm leaving my last class of the day with Teagan, you would have thought I was Kanye West.

"Oh my god! Marley! You and David! So cute!" Taylor P. yells in my face along with ten other girls.

Embarrassed by the attention, Teagan and I make a run for it to my locker.

"This isn't happening," I say to Teagan.

"It is. You and David are now the Love and Basketball of the school." She laughs.

"Not funny," I respond, glaring at her.

I'm so unhappy right now. Everyone's celebrating this relationship, and I'm the one in it. It's been two hours, and I'm miserable. We walk to our bus lines. My bus has already arrived, so I hug Teagan bye and run out.

As soon as I sit down on the bus, I check my phone.

Jess (3:08 p.m.): hey superstar

Okay, maybe Dakota's bullhorn wasn't too bad.

Me (3:09 p.m.): haha, stop.

Jess (3:10 p.m.): hahah you're too cool for me now

Me (3:12 p.m.): lol. No I'm not.

Jess (3:14 p.m.): we'll see

Me (3:16 p.m.): stop! You're my best friend!

Me (3:16 p.m.): which I have to tell you something

Me (3:17 p.m.): nothing crazy, but it's spreading like a wildfire

Jess (3:18 p.m.): you're my best friend too. don't tell Dani. What's going on?

Dani is Jess's *other* best friend.

Ugh, I don't know why I'm so nervous to tell her.

Me (3:23 p.m.): so after the assembly David asked me out :]

Jess (3:27 p.m.): oh?

Oh? What the hell do I say to "Oh?"

Jess (3:28 p.m.): Did you say yes? I didn't know you liked him

Me (3:34 p.m.): I mean he's cute, right?

Jess (3:42 p.m.): sure I guess. I have tennis, ttyl. Good luck at your game.

Me (3:43 p.m.): okay... Thanks.

Well, damn. Okay.

That didn't exactly go as planned. Jess seems pretty weird about the whole deal. In her defense, I've never talked about David, probably because I don't like him or maybe I kind of do; I don't know yet. So her feelings on the matter are pretty much justified.

When I get home, I check MySpace.

"Dear god, you people are crazy," I say aloud.

They're writing on my page about this four-hour-old relationship. Is this what my life has become? I scroll through the posts when my direct messages notifies me.

David (online now): hey

Okay, let try this out.

Me (online now): hey

David (online now): how ru?

Me (online now): good. Just got home but will have to go soon since I have a game.

David (online now): oh. You see those posts? Haha

Me (online now): yeah. They're crazy haha

David (online now): right :)

Hmm, do I like him? I mean, he's not my first boyfriend, but I don't know. Something about it feels off.

I talk to David for the next hour. It's a good conversation. We get to know each other a little bit. Something we probably should have done before jumping into a relationship, but, you know, junior high. I keep checking my phone to see if I have any messages from Jess even though I know she's at tennis. The only ones are my group text with only Dakota blowing me up to see what my married life is like. Everyone's acting like I haven't been in a relationship before. Does third grade count? I did date a guy in my neighborhood last year, too. Maybe because this is my first since we've become teenagers, so it's more "real" or something. I don't know. Anyway, it's starting to annoy me.

I log off so I can get ready for my game. I have a million and one things running through my head.

"Mar, are you ready to go?" my sister Kendal asks me.

"Yeah, give me two minutes," I reply.

I grab my uniform from my closet and place it in my bag. I check my phone one last time making sure I didn't miss a text from Jess.

Nothing.

Letting out a sigh, I grab my bag and head for the car. Mom drives me to the school and reminds me of everything I need to do when I get home and for the rest of my life.

We arrive at the gym, and I see Teagan getting out of her car, walking to the doors. I hop out to catch her.

"T!" I yell.

She turns around. "Mar! You ready?!"

I walk up to her. "Yeah, I guess so."

"What's wrong?" she asks.

"Nothing. I think just nerves," I reply, lying.

"Well, put on your game face," she says, smiling, throwing her arm over my shoulder.

I smile and roll my eyes at her.

We make our way inside only to learn we're on the wrong side of the building. While Teagan is looking for a way to the other side without going back outside to walk around the entire campus, I check my phone again.

Nothing.

"Mar, stop," I whisper to myself as I shove my phone back into my bag.

"Find anything helpful?" I ask Teagan, who's peeking inside classroom windows.

"Not yet," she answers.

"Well, T, I really don't think what you're doing is helping the situation. Let's just walk around outside before we miss our own game," I say, opening the doors to outside.

"Ugh, fine, but I was getting there. I saw a map in that classroom, and I was trying to read it!" she says, snatching her bag off the ground.

I laugh and shake my head. "Come on."

The game was really fun. I was able to get my mind off of David and Jess with the help of Teagan and her craziness. Although there were times in the game when Jess may or may not have popped into my head. I think I'm just sad that she seems to be upset with me. Maybe she feels as if I kept liking David a secret from her. Well, *like* is a strong word because I really never thought about David until Dakota brought him up today. I guess if it were Teagan, I'd feel some type of way too, not knowing she liked someone and just hopped into a relationship.

We stop for ice cream on the way home. I order my favorite: peppermint.

"You played great, Mar," Mom says, handing me my cone.

I grab it, licking the sides of melting ice cream. "Thanks, Mom!" I reply.

"You did okay. I've seen better," Kendal adds.

I grab her cone from Mom. "I'll throw it out!" I tease, rolling down the window.

"Stop, I'm joking," she says, reaching for it.

I hand it to her. "I thought so."

Instinctively, I check my phone again.

"Marley, you've looked at that phone a hundred times since we left the gym!" Mom says, giving me a crazy look. "Don't forget you have things to do when we get home. Do I need to take it from you until you've finished your homework and picked up your room?"

Yikes! I can't have that.

I begin to respond, "I um—"

"Marley has a boyfriend now!" Kendal yells from the back seat.

Why can't I ever have a peaceful day, Lord?

Mom hits the brakes. "What?! Since when?!"

"It's no big deal, Mom," I reply.

I reach my arm behind my seat to punch Kendal in the knee. "Ow!" she squeals.

"Marley, cut it out, and, yes, it is a big deal! Who is he?" she asks.

I put my hand on my forehead. "His name is David Johnson. He plays on the boys' basketball team."

Mom begins driving again. "Hmm, I will need to meet Mr. David," she replies.

I glance at her. "Mom, we aren't getting married!"

"You might!" Kendal says.

"Shut up, Kendal!" I grunt.

"Hey, none of that!" Mom says, pointing her finger at me.

How am I the one to get in trouble when Kendal has a fat mouth? Younger siblings have it bad. Pray for us.

Anyway, as we pull into the driveway, my phone buzzes. I flip it over, hoping to see Jess' name across the screen.

Blah.

It's Dakota texting the team.

Dakota (8:17 p.m.): Good job, ladies!

Before I can respond, Mom grabs my phone.

My jaw drops, but I can't say, "What the hell?" unless I want to be punted into next week.

"You'll get it back once you finish your homework and pick up your room," she says, placing it in her purse.

I sigh quietly to myself and get out the car. Mom has a two-door sports car, so I shut the passenger door in Kendal's face and make my way inside.

I take a quick shower.

"Ah," I say as I jump on my bed.

I reach into my backpack to grab my math book. "Okay, let's do this," I say.

Ten minutes in, I'm confused. I want to text Jess about it, but I think she's clearly mad at me since she hasn't talked to me all evening.

Ugh, I don't want to be annoying, but I do need help.

I walk to the kitchen to ask for my phone.

"Hey, Mom, can I have my phone for ten minutes? I need help with my math," I say, smiling innocently.

She gives me a look. "You have ten minutes, Marley."

I smile from ear to ear.

She goes over to her purse to grab it. "Thanks!" I say as I run back to my room.

I shut my door and plop on the bed.

I have a text from David, but I ignore it for now. Still no text from Jess.

Here goes nothin'.

Me (9:45 p.m.): Jess?

Jess (9:46 p.m.): yeah?

Ouch.

Me (9:46 p.m.): you're mad aren't you.

Jess (9:47 p.m.): not mad

Me (9:47 p.m.): what do you call it?

Jess (9:47 p.m.): idk

Right, not mad.

Me (9:48 p.m.): I do like him. He's cool.

Jess (9:48 p.m.): That's great Marley.

Me (9:49 p.m.): so what's wrong with you

Jess (9:50 p.m.): nothing is wrong

Me (9:51 p.m.): right. Okay then Jess.

Jess (9:52 p.m.): going to bed. See you tomorrow.

So much for help with math.

Me (9:53 p.m.): K.

Great. Just great. Tomorrow should be fun, and I say this with one hundred percent sarcasm.

Chapter 4

Waking up, I remember that today will suck. I am absolutely dreading going to art. I should feel like a queen today. We won our game last night and I went from single to taken. Yay, right? Well, I don't feel like a queen, and that reminds me...I forgot to text David back last night. Oops.

The bus ride to school feels like I'm on my way to a funeral. I ask my fairy godmother if she'd pop a tire or miraculously make us run out of gas. I don't get those wishes granted. As we pull into the school, I can feel my heart rate increasing. I look out the window to see if I can see Teagan's bus.

Ugh, I don't.

My phone buzzes.

Teagan (7:21 a.m.): Mar you won't believe this!

What could possibly be happening this early?

Me (7:21 a.m.): What's up T?

Teagan (7:22 a.m.): Our bus driver ran over something and blew a tire! :O I almost flew out the window! P.S won't be at breakfast

You. Have. Got. To. Be. Kidding. Me.

Me (7:22 a.m.): No way.

Teagan (7:23 a.m.): Yes way! We are waiting on another bus to come pick us up

I look up to the bus ceiling. "Wow."

I make my way off the bus and to the cafeteria. While I wait in line, I put my earbuds in so I don't feel awkward standing in line by myself. I still haven't texted David back from last night and Jess still hasn't texted me. She usually says good morning. That's how I know she's pissed at me.

I feel a tap on my shoulder.

"Hey, Marley."

I turn around to see David. "Hey," I say with an awkward smile. "Sorry I didn't text you back. I had to do homework."

"It's okay. Whatcha bout to eat?" he asks, grabbing his ID card.

"David and Marley sitting in a tree!" I hear Dakota yelling in the distance.

"Kill me now," I say to David.

He laughs. "I don't know how people make things such a big deal."

"Right?" I say as I move forward in line.

"Hey, guys!" Dakota says, leaning over the railing.

"Hey, D," I respond.

"What are we doing?" she says with a devilish smile.

I glance at the food and back to Dakota. "Um, getting breakfast?"

"I see that, Marley, I mean—"

I look over and see Jess walking with Dani. We make eye contact and I look back over at Dakota. I tune her back in.

"So?" she asks.

"So what?" I reply.

"Were you even listening to me, Marley?!"

Lying, I reply, "Um, yes."

"Let's grab our food," David says, gesturing me toward the hot bar.

"Gotta go, my boyfriend would like to eat breakfast," I say jokingly.

I immediately regret saying "boyfriend." I don't like the way it came off my tongue, kind of like it tasted gross.

We grab our breakfast and make our way inside the cafeteria. I feel like all eyes are on us. *Teagan, please hurry.*

We're following Dakota to a table. I have no idea why because she doesn't have any food, but okay, I guess.

"Let's sit with my friend Dani...Dani!" she yells across the room.

You've got to be kidding me.

Do I have bad luck? Did I do something to piss off Karma?

We walk over. Dani stands and waves to Dakota. I glance at Jess, and she looks like, "What the hell is happening?" Even though I'm mad at her for being mad at me, I laugh in my head. Jess isn't really fond of Dakota.

She grows on you...kinda.

"Marley, you sit there!" Dakota says, gesturing for me to sit in front of Jess, which leaves David sitting in front of Dani.

"Um, okay," I say as I place my tray down, avoiding eye contact with Jess.

David sits down and waves to them both. "Hey," he says.

"Hi," Jess replies.

She glances at me and I look down at my food.

"David, right?" Dani asks.

Dakota butts in, "Back off, Dani, he's taken by Marley!"

"Really?" I say, shaking my head.

"I'm just messing around; don't get your panties in a wad," she replies.

I shake my head and open my applesauce.

"You're crazy!" Dani says, playfully pushing Dakota. "Aren't they so cute?" she asks Jess.

I look up at Dani, then Jess, and back to Dani. Jess is uncomfortable, I'm uncomfortable, and David is uncomfortable. I'll call it.

"Ya know, I think I'm gonna head to class," I say standing, putting my applesauce back on the tray.

"Me too," David adds. "I'll take this for you." He grabs my tray.

"Thanks," I say, smirking. "Oh wait," I say as I grab my chocolate milk.

David laughs. "Don't want to waste a good chocolate milk."

"Exactly," I reply.

David walks off and I reach down to grab my backpack. I mistakenly glance up to see Dakota and Dani staring at me, smiling.

"Oh god," I say, putting on my backpack. Jess is on her phone, not texting me back. "See you guys," I say, walking off.

"Bye, Marley Johnson!" Dakota yells.

Is it too late to transfer schools?

Ugh, that was the worst. Jess is the worst...

Okay, she's not, but I'm getting a major cold shoulder right now, so she is the worst, temporarily. Also, was this my first breakfast date? If we're counting it, then it was definitely the worst first breakfast date in the history of breakfast dates.

I'd rather not think about it. I make my way to my first-hour class.

I honestly don't know what any teacher had to say in any of my morning classes. I had one thing on my mind: Jess. Just because she's mad at me, of course—no other reason. Lunch is extremely boring and uncomfortable without Teagan. I need it to go by fast and slow. Fast, because I can't listen to another word come out of Dakota's mouth, and slow because my next class is art. *Ugh.* Can this constitute as the worst day of my life?

After the bell rings, I run as far away from Dakota as possible. Jess and I usually meet each other at the stairs to walk to art together. Something tells me that won't be happening today. I skip the meeting spot and head straight to art. I go in and take my seat next to Laura.

"Hey, Marley," she says.

I glance over at her. "Hey."

"Someone's in a mood," she says, raising her glasses.

Jess walks in and sits next to me. It's her assigned seat; I'm sure if she could change, she would have.

I look over at her and shake my head. She really isn't budging. I kind of get it. She told me right away about Sam and how hot he is. She is justified, I suppose.

Mr. Blake walks up to his podium.

"Okay, class, today we'll be working outside," he begins. "With your groups, you will recreate our school, each painting a different portion of the building," he says, passing out mini easels.

"Have you seen Brandon?" I ask Laura.

"I don't think he's here today. I usually see him at lunch," she replies.

Mr. Blake walks up to us.

"Laura, do you mind partnering with Sadie today? We have a few students out today due to a bus mishap," he asks, handing her an easel.

"Of course I will," she says, standing. "See ya guys!" She waves to me and Jess.

And then there were two.

Mr. Blake hands us both an easel.

"Ladies, the supplies are at the front on the way out," he says. "Oh, and great game last night, Marley."

"Thank you, Mr. Blake."

"Okay, thank you," Jess replies.

To be quite honest, I'm trying my absolute hardest to be mad at Jess and I just can't. I want to be mad at her so bad for this silent treatment she's giving me, and I just can't. Why?

We make our way outside. Jess has been walking next to me since we left the classroom, but she isn't talking to me.

"We can sit over there," I say, pointing to a curb in front of the school. Jess follows me over.

We sit and set up shop. Jess sits about three feet away from me. I let out a sigh.

"Jess," I say, looking over to her.

She looks at me. The sun is shining in her eyes. I have to look away immediately.

She grabs her paintbrush. "What?"

"How are we going to do this if you aren't talking to me?" I ask, grabbing my brush.

She shrugs.

Screw this.

I grab her paintbrush. "Please stop."

She sighs and folds her arms.

"I didn't tell you about David because there was nothing to tell," I begin. "I just found out yesterday that he liked me, and he asked me out on the spot, so I said yes."

She turns to me. "So do you like him?"

"I'm not sure. He's cool and really nice," I reply, shrugging.

"Hmm," she says, squinting her eyes at me.

I start mixing paint. "Aren't you tired of fighting me?"

"No," she says, smiling.

Of course, I smile back.

"I almost texted you good morning and I stopped myself," she says, moving closer to me now that we're friends again.

"Oh, no, stay over there, Jess," I joke.

She stops. "Fine."

I shake my head. "Jess, you give me headaches."

Mr. Blake walks over. "Hey, ladies, how are we doing?"

"I'm doing okay; I don't think Jess knows what she's doing, though," I say jokingly.

Jess makes a surprised face at me.

"Now, now, I'm sure you both are doing just fine. We have about twenty minutes before we need to pack up," he says, walking to the next group.

Jess takes her paintbrush and strokes my arm.

"Wow!" I say, chuckling.

"That's for that and being mean," she says, smiling.

"You know what? Fine," I reply, smirking.

We finish our painting. Mine is horrid compared to Jess'. She's a great artist. The rest of the afternoon, I walk the halls as if I've won the lottery. I'm so happy Jess isn't mad at me anymore. I knew she was going to budge in class because that's when we have one-on-one time. She can't resist her best friend. I mean, c'mon, it's Marley Waters we're talking about. Just kidding. I'm great but not that great.

Okay, I'm that great.

After the last bell, I prepare to make a run for my bus while I'm ahead. Unfortunately, I'm not out of the dark side yet.

"Hey, Marley!" I hear David call behind me.

Dammit.

Honestly, junior high relationships are weird. What is the point of them? Do I even like David?

"Oh, hey, man," I reply.

I look awkwardly from side to side.

"You want me to walk you to your bus?" he asks.

"Um, okay…sure," I say, walking toward the stairs.

"Should we hold hands?" he asks, grinning.

Oh, wow.

"Okay," I reply, stretching out my hand.

"Ooo, Marley!" I hear from several classmates as we're making our way to the buses.

This is the worst. Please don't run into Dakota.

As we're walking, I tilt my head down slightly as if it makes me incognito. I'm not embarrassed by David. He's really cool. I just...I don't know.

David walks me all the way to the bus door entrance. I can only think that he's trying to make it to second base: a kiss.

"This is me," I say with an awkward smile.

"Nice ride," he replies.

I laugh. I like his sense of humor. "Super stretch limo. One of a kind."

"I guess I'll see you tomorrow. Do you want to meet at breakfast like we did today?" he asks, bending down to tie his shoe.

"Um, sure, that's cool," I reply.

"Nice. Okay, awesome," he smiles.

"Okay, well, see ya," I say.

"Can I give you a—"

Oh, please don't say it.

"Hug?" He opens his arms.

I look around to see if anyone is watching. "Okay," I say, taking a step forward.

He throws his arms around me gently and holds me for maybe three seconds. It feels like three years, and I can feel my body overheating. I know I'm turning red. I hug him back and quickly let go.

"Okay, see you tomorrow!" I say, hurrying onto my bus.

"Ooo!" my friend Tyler says as I walk on.

"Shut up," I grunt.

I sigh and plop down in a seat and put my hoodie on top of my head.

I begin wallowing in my sorrows. I look down at my arm and see the paint mark Jess gave me in art. I smile. I take out my phone to send her a text.

Me (3:13 p.m.): Hope you have a lawyer

I tuck my phone back in my pocket and rest my head on the window. I wake to Tyler yelling at me to get off the bus; we are at my stop.

"What are you doing? Daydreaming about your boyfriend?" he says, jumping off the last step.

"You're dead!" I say as I chase him through our neighbors' yards.

I chase him six houses down before he surrenders. "Okay, okay!" he yells, dropping to the ground.

"You're getting faster," I say, offering my hand.

He grabs it and pulls himself up. "Thanks. I want to run track next year," he says, breathing heavily.

Tyler is in the sixth grade, by the way.

"So when did you get a boyfriend?" he asks as we walk back to our houses.

"Yesterday," I reply.

"Oh. Cool."

"Yep," I say, wishing he'd change the subject.

He looks over to me. "You never talk about boys. I didn't know you liked a boy."

I glance at him and keep walking.

I mean, he has a point. I don't talk about boys. It's just not something I do. Most girls sit around rating guys all day long and I couldn't care less. I mean, I don't talk about girls, either. Well, that's weird, anyway, right? I just don't talk about anything that involves stuff like that. I'd rather talk about sports or something. Anything besides relationships.

I change the subject and tell him to come outside later. We head home.

I get inside and run straight into the kitchen. I need a snack.

My phone buzzes.

Jess (3:46 p.m.): Hahah and why is that?

I smile and hop on the counter.

My worries for the day leave as I engage in a nice, friendly conversation with Jess. She's my absolute most favorite human being in the world.

Chapter 5

Thanksgiving break starts in less than ten minutes, and I'm actually excited to have a two-week break to lay on my couch and do absolutely nothing but watch TV. I'm also excited because I get to talk to Jess all day, every day, without school interrupting. Oh, and David. Ha.

Jess and Sam are dating now. This didn't sit well with Teagan, and I don't know what to think about everything. Ever since they started dating, Dani has been clinging to Jess for dear life. That makes me wonder what Dani expects from Jess, I smell a little jealousy. Well, I can't talk. Anyway, Jess tells me she's happy with Sam and that's he's sweet and kind. That's how I describe David, my boyfriend extraordinaire.

"Marley, Mar!" Teagan shouts across the hall.

"T, you ready for Thanksgiving break?" I respond.

"Hell yeah," she says, grabbing her backpack out her locker.

"Marley!" I turn around to see Taylor P.

"Oh, hey, Taylor, what's up?"

"Everyone's going to the movies tonight; spread the word," she says.

"What movie? *Yes Man*?" I ask, slightly excited because I've been waiting to see it.

"Really, Marley, you child. We don't know yet. Just be there, okay?" she says, walking away.

"Sir, yes, sir. If my mom will let me," I say under my breath.

"What was that about?" Teagan asks.

"Movies tonight. You think you can go?" I ask her.

"Maybe; will have to ask," she says.

"Same," I say, walking to the bus lines.

I text my mom asking if I can go to the movies. Of course, I have to get the movie time information, what it's rated, who's in it, who's going, everyone's Social Security number, what mall, what time it ends, and I can't be a minute late with my curfew. And, no, my mom isn't kidding. I honestly didn't play any games either because I absolutely cannot afford to lose my phone the day Thanksgiving break starts.

Me (3:29 p.m.): you going to this movie thing tonight?

Jess (3:30 p.m.): maybe, who's asking?

Me (3:32 p.m.): haha really...me.

Jess (3:35 p.m.): well in that case

Jess (3:35 p.m.): maybe

Me (3:37 p.m.): hahah ok, see you there

Jess (3:39 p.m.): I didn't say I was going. Was supposed to hang with sam tonight.

Me (3:45 p.m.): oh… well don't worry about it then

Jess (3:46 p.m.): can I bring him?

Me (3:48 p.m.): who am I the movie police?

Jess (3:51 p.m.): hahah, shutup

Me (3:53 p.m.): lol, see you guys there

Jess (3:55 p.m.): oh you're done texting?

Me (3:57 p.m.): my mom is going to do my hair before tonight. Black girl probs.

Jess (3:59 p.m.): hahah shutup Marley. Getting dolled up for David I see. :)

Me (4:06 p.m.): lol bye Jess.

Honestly, I don't know who I'm getting dolled up for. Is it for David or is it for Jess? I feel weird. I stop thinking about it.

"So, who's going to this thing?" my mom asks as she's braiding my hair.

"I think a few friends from 701 and 702," I answer.

"Okay. Act up if you want to," she barks.

"I'm not crazy, Mom," I say as my phone buzzes.

Teagan (4:47 p.m.): Peeps!

Dakota (4:47 p.m.): yall goin?

Teagan (4:48p .m.): my mom said yes what about yall

Dakota (4:49 p.m.): mine too. mar?

Me (4:51 p.m.): yeah I'm good to go! I just want to know what we're seeing!

Dakota (4:52 p.m.): Marley, you wont be watching cuz youll be kissing on David!

I'm sorry, what? Probably not. I don't know why I don't break up with him. I really only see him as a good friend.

Me (4:53 p.m.): whoa, no. none of that. I just want to hang with friends.

Dakota (4:54 p.m.): but you have a boyfriend

Teagan (4:55 p.m.): D, why don't we let Marley handle her relationship

Dakota (4:57 p.m.): whatever.

The best thing to do when it comes to Dakota is to ignore her mess.

Me (4:58 p.m.): let me know when y'all are about to leave.

As the time gets closer to 7 p.m., nerves begin to set in. I'm not sure why, but in the back of my mind, I am truly only excited to hang out with Jess or be in the same space as her since no one knows we're good friends. Maybe. She's bringing her boyfriend, so I'm not sure how this will play out.
Shit. So am I.
Anyway, of course I'm excited to hang with the rest of my friends, but I am also dreading hanging with David. Is he expecting this to be some make out session? God, I hope not.
"Thanks, Mom," I say, getting out the car. "Be ready at ten-thirty."

Here I go. *Oh, dear god, why am I here?* Immediate regret.

Me (7:07 p.m.): you guys here?

I start walking inside the mall to wait on Teagan and Dakota. I am extremely uncomfortable and nervous to be walking by myself. I don't want to run into David or Jess.

Teagan (7:07 p.m.): getting out the car now

There is a god. I turn around mid-step and run back outside to Teagan. She tells her mom goodbye, and we sit outside the mall to wait for Dakota.

"You ready to see David?" Teagan asks.

"Honestly, I'm not sure," I reply.

"I know you don't like him like that, Mar, why are you dating him?" she says as she watches for Dakota's mom's car.

I sit there silent and watch for cars with her. I also receive a text from David.

David (7:29 p.m.): u there?

I don't respond...

"Hey, bitches!" Dakota yells as her mom pulls away.

Teagan and I give each other a look. "What's up, D," I say.

"Hey, girl, hey," Teagan says, unamused.

"Marley, are you ready to kiss David?" Dakota asks.

I'm already annoyed and she's been in my presence for thirty seconds. "Damn, Dakota, do *you* want to kiss David?" I snap.

"Shut up, Marley!" she says and laughs maliciously.

We walk into the mall, and I can immediately smell Auntie Anne's pretzels. Those make you weak in the knees

and forget all your worries. If you haven't had one, *go now.*
The closer we get to the food court, the more I grow nervous.
Do I look okay? Did I put deodorant on? Is my hair ugly?
I can't stop asking myself these questions. I have no idea
what Teagan and Dakota were talking about on the way
over. Before we get to the escalator, I hear a familiar voice
call my name.

"Marley!"

We turn around to see David. Yes, woo, my boyfriend.
I should be happier than this, right?

"Oh, hey, David," I say in my best "excited" voice.

"I wonder what movie they're trying to see," he responds,
checking out my outfit.

God, now I hope I look okay for David. I just watched
him check me out. I'm going to be sick.

"Oh, by the way, you look great," he adds.

Teagan and Dakota react as if he just recited his wedding
vows to me. I give them a look.

"Thanks. So do you," I say.

I mean, he looks nice. He definitely made an effort since
this is our first hangout outside of school. I don't know;
whatever.

We get onto the escalator and I can see our friends over
by the movie ticket booth. I feel like I am going to pass out.
We are the last ones to arrive, so all eyes are on us. It's a fate
I can never escape, apparently. A few of the girls let out their
*ooo*s and *ahh*s at David and me.

As we get closer, I skim the crowd to find Jess standing
with Dani and Sam. She looks absolutely stunning. Her hair
is straightened, pulled back with a white headband, and she

is wearing a black dress with a white jacket. She has a small pink-and-white clutch purse that she's holding in her left hand. She and Sam are sharing a pretzel. Cute.

To get to the ticket booth to pay for our tickets, we have to pass them. I'm actually sick at this point. No one really knows we're friends—best friends at that. Do I speak? Do I wave? What do I do, Lord?

"Dani!" Dakota yells, startling me.

Dakota runs to Dani, picks her up, and gives her a hug. I didn't know they were such good friends.

Jess and I make eye contact and smirk with confusion. We usually smile at each other when we make eye contact. I don't know, it's a thing even though I can barely look at her half the time.

While Dakota is being Dakota, talking to Dani, I catch Jess sneakily check out David and look back at me. I immediately look away and start talking to Teagan.

"We should probably grab our tickets."

"Yeah, everyone is waiting on us," she says. "D, come on."

I run over to Taylor P. to ask her what movie we're going to see. "So, what's the verdict, TP?" I ask.

"Don't you dare, Marley!" she says shoving me. "And what do you think? The only movie we *can* see," she says, rolling her eyes.

I smile because I know what that means. *Yes Man*. Ahh, great movie.

"Stop smiling and go get your tickets," she says, pushing me toward the booth.

"Yes, captain," I say sarcastically. I get the crew and we start for the ticket booth.

"I got us," David says.

"You got what? I can—"

"Say whaaat?! You're paying for all of us?!" Dakota says, interrupting me.

"Yeah," David replies, smiling at me.

"Oh, you don't have to do that, David. Seriously, I can pay for myself," I say, pulling out my wallet.

"No, really, I got us. Do y'all want to grab the popcorn while I pay?" he says, pulling a wad of one-dollar bills from his pocket.

"Okay, sure," I respond.

Teagan, Dakota, and I walk over to the concession stand. My phone buzzes.

Jess (7:46 p.m.): hey

I can't help but smile. I look over my shoulder for Dakota and Teagan because the last thing I need is for Dakota to know I'm real friends with Jess, like the textable kind of friends. Not just friends at school…well, technically, we only are. Whatever. Anyway, I don't mind if Teagan knows, but at this point she doesn't, and I'm okay with that. Fewer questions and avoidable interrogations. Plus, I'd hate to be caught smiling at her text messages, and they ask me why I'm smiling at her saying absolutely nothing but "hey." I wouldn't have an answer to give them.

Me (7:48 p.m.): aren't you on a date?

Jess (7:48 p.m.): aren't you?

Me (7:49 p.m.): Touche. What's up?

Wait, did I just call this a date?

"Marley!" Teagan yells. Apparently, she's been yelling my name for the past two minutes.

"Huh, yeah?" I reply.

"Well, it's too late now. I had them put butter on your popcorn. If you don't like it, I'll eat it," she says as she grabs a handful of my popcorn.

"Gee, thank you so much, T," I say sarcastically.

Everyone from the group starts walking toward us. I haven't checked my phone to see if Jess texted back.

"Are we ready?" Taylor P. asks.

"As far as I know," I say with a shrug.

Jess and I make eye contact for a split second and look away. I smile to myself and start walking with the group.

Have you ever had a soft spot for someone who makes you smile when you see them? And you don't even realize you're smiling? Jess is my soft spot, I am coming to realize.

I take a quick glance at my phone before we walk into the theater.

Jess (7:50 p.m.): let's sit by each other

Holy shit. Okay. How can I pull this off?

I know what you're thinking. Marley, just say you want to sit by her; it's not a big deal. Oh, but it is a big deal.

Remember when I told you what I do or say will be used against me in the court of law? Well, this is what I mean. I have to be so strategic because in the later years, this could come back to bite me in the ass. And at the end of the day, I don't want to make Jess uncomfortable. I don't want to run her off.

Here we go. I was made for this.

"Come on, guys," I say to the crew. "Let's get to the front so we can pick good seats."

Yep, made that up. I'm getting too good at this secret life.

"Yeah, I don't want somebody's big head in my way," Dakota adds, power walking to the front of the group.

Ahh, operation finesse is in full effect.

"Wait up!" Teagan yells, holding two bags of popcorn, M&Ms, a hot dog, and a large Icee.

"T, why in the world did you buy all of that?" I turn around, laughing.

"It all sounded so good, so I just got it all," she says as popcorn spills to the floor.

Crap. Where's David? I turn around to look for him and see him laughing and playing with his teammates. Thank god.

We arrive at the theater's doors. There are literally like twenty of us and parents are immediately annoyed. The twenty-four-year-old me would be too, probably. Loud-ass kids.

"Where should we sit?" I say, playing along to my own plan of finesse.

"The middle, for sure!" Dakota says, running to the stairs. Dani overhears Dakota saying that.

"Okay, it's four of us, so we just need four seats," I say to Teagan.

"On it," Teagan replies, running after Dakota.

David catches up to me at the same time Jess catches up to me. She gives him a look that he doesn't see, but I do. It makes me laugh to myself. Do I smell jealousy? Not that kind; the friendship kind. I was jealous of Sam. The friendship kind, of course.

"Okay, Teagan and Dakota are grabbing the seats," I say to David.

"Okay, cool," he says, walking up the aisle.

I slip behind David to have him walk in front of me. Jess, Dani, and Sam are behind me.

"Hey, Marley," I hear behind me. Glancing at Jess, Dani waves for my attention.

"Hey..." I say with a confused look.

"Are you guys planning on sitting in the middle? I really like the middle," she says.

Operation finesse is running so smoothly. I entertain her.

"Well, yeah, but there's plenty of seats in the row. You guys can sit next to us," I say with a small smile.

Jess grins.

I glance at Sam. Damn, He's a pretty cute white boy. Shaggy brown hair. The classic 2008 twelve-year-old look. Bleh. I continue walking.

"Mar, over here," Dakota yells.

I look up to see they have a spot for me between Teagan and David. Shit. Okay, play it cool, Marley.

"Here, Mar," Teagan says.

I'm quick thinking on my feet. "How about David sits there? That way I'm closer to the stairs. I have a feeling my drink is going to have me running to the bathroom nonstop," I say, trying to keep a "playing it cool" face.

"Yeah, stay over there. I don't need you distracting me the whole time," Dakota adds.

Operation finesse is a success. Damn, I'm tired now. That was a rough five minutes.

Jess sits down next to me. "Oh, sorry, this seat is taken," I say to her.

She smiles.

This is the first time I have the guts to look at her longer than two seconds, and damn, it is a sight to see. I smile back.

"Oh, sorry. Let me find a new one," she says as she places her Icee in the cup holder.

"Looks like you're getting comfortable instead," I say, trying not to sound flirtatious.

"I am," she says, looking at me with her mind-boggling hazelnut eyes.

I am mesmerized. I smile and turn away so I don't look like a creep. I start talking to the crew before the movie begins.

"I'm actually excited to see this movie," David says, gesturing at his bag of popcorn.

"So am I," I respond, showing him my bag.

We laugh. He's clearly nervous. Honestly, so am I.

Dakota is eating her popcorn as if it's her last meal, making a complete mess. I hope she has napkins.

The lights dim. The previews start playing. I don't know why, but my heart starts pounding. I'm not sure if it's from me thinking David is going to try to kiss me or the fact that I'm sitting beside Jess and our friendship is incognito.

My phone buzzes. My light is bright, causing Jess to look at me and then down at my phone.

Dakota (8:11 p.m.): soooooo

I begin to respond and Jess nudges me. "That's not bright at all," she says with a smirk on her face.

"Sorry," I reply with a smile.

"Don't let it happen again," she says jokingly.

I laugh and go back to my phone, dimming the light as low as I can.

Me (8:12 p.m.): we aren't doing this. Bye D!

My phone buzzes again but it isn't Dakota.

David (8:13 p.m.): srry if im blowing this. Im nervous.

Ugh.

My phone buzzes again.

Jess (8:14 p.m.): are you going to be a distraction? I'll have to report you to security.

I can't help but smile once again.

Me (8:14 p.m. to Jess): oh so you're the movie police? Double agent. Nice.

I glance over at Jess after I send it and see her smiling at her phone. Was it to my message? She could be texting Sam, too. I don't know.

Me (8:15 p.m. to David): haha you're fine, David. We're all just hanging out.

The movie starts and as much as I want to pay attention, my mind is all over the place. I have my *boyfriend* sitting next to me and my secret best friend sitting next to me. The more

I think about it, I have no idea why we are a secret. I mean, we're just friends, after all. It is overwhelming, to say the least, but as you can guess, I like it. The suspense of it all is my kryptonite.

I don't know why my friendship with Jess is different than Teagan's and mine, being as though they are both technically my best friends—okay, and Dakota, even though she gets on my nerves. But I don't look at Teagan or Dakota, or anyone, for that matter—the way I look at Jess. I don't know. I don't know what's wrong with me.

My drink actually did end up catching up to me, so now I have to contemplate getting up in front of everyone. If I do get up, I have no choice but to go Jess's way because of the crap I made up earlier. Man. I really hate having all eyes on me. I wonder if I can hold it.

Yeah, nope. Dammit.

I tell David I'll be back. He insists on coming and I kindly decline. I start to get up and Jess looks at me. *Dear god, stop looking at me; it makes me die inside.* She gives me a confused look and I mouth "bathroom" and start climbing over everyone's legs. Once I leave the theater, I really don't want to go back in. I feel like I can't breathe again. I'm convinced they tampered with the oxygen output in there.

Anyway, I make my way to the bathroom.

Jess (9:47 p.m.): are you okay?

Me (9:52 p.m.): haha yeah. I drank a little too much.

Jess (9:54 p.m.): you might want to hurry or you'll miss the end

I plan on going back in until I see an arcade.

Me (9:59 p.m.): it's okay. I actually see an arcade calling my name. :)

Jess (10:00 p.m.): haha you're crazy

I grab a Snickers bar from the concession stand and walk over to the arcade. I wouldn't have guessed this is where I would be right now, but I'm not mad about it. I traded a few of my dollars in for quarters and went to town. I feel at peace and I'm really happy.

Unfortunately, it doesn't last long.

"Hey, Marley," I hear David call.

"Hey. Sorry I bailed. I saw this arcade and couldn't resist," I reply.

"It's all good. It was terrifying in there anyway," he says, taking out a few dollars.

David is really cool. But like, as a friend or a brother. We get along really well; I just don't see him like *that*. I really need to break up with him.

"Best out of three?" I say to him, walking to the basketball machine.

"Yeah, don't get your hopes up," he says, laughing, starting the game.

We play more than three games. More like twelve. After the twelfth game, he starts telling me how much fun he had and that he wasn't surprised I kicked his ass. I let him know I had fun too. We walk over to this random ice cream vending machine in the corner of the arcade and I put my money in for some cookies and crème Dippin' Dots. Yum.

As I come up from grabbing the ice cream, he grabs my face and kisses me.

"*Oh my god!*" Dakota screams from across the theater lobby.

I freeze. *No way.* What the hell type of timing is this? Strike me dead, god.

Everyone starts their *ooo*s and *ahh*s, and I've never been more embarrassed. I immediately turn red. David is smiling and I am not. I'm searching the crowd for Jess. Why? I don't know; that was my first instinct.

Jess is standing next to Dani and Sam, talking. She isn't facing us directly. Did she not see? I'm going to throw up. Before I can think of my next move, I realize the movie is over, considering everyone is now in front of me, and I have a curfew to be in that parking lot at ten thirty and not a minute late. I look down at the time and see it's 10:27.

Oh, shit.

"I gotta go like right now," I tell the crew frantically.

I take off sprinting for the exit. Jess looks at me as I run by looking like I'd just robbed a bank. I have less than two minutes to have my ass at the car or I am done for, so I have no time for absolutely anything. Bad timing to take off sprinting, to say the least, but I have no time for explanations.

I feel like I'm in *Bad Boys*. I bust out a pair of exit doors, run down a creepy side alley next to the building, and climb over a small wall leading to the parking lot. My Dippin' Dots don't survive such action. I see my mom's car in the distance, and I run like I've never run before.

I am running for Jess.

Chapter 6

Thanksgiving break went as well as one could imagine. By the way, I made curfew thanks to my supersonic speed. I think Mom gave me a pass because I was sprinting across the parking lot as if my life depended on it.

Talking to Jess the entire break was the most fun I had, and I played outside a lot, which is *fun fun,* so imagine how much fun I had talking to my most favorite person in the world twenty-four-seven. I oddly found myself checking my phone every second for her messages while also hoping not to see David's messages pop up on my screen. I didn't bring up the kiss to Jess; I'm just hoping she didn't see it. If she did, I guess we're both just hanging out with the elephant because neither of us have said anything.

When we get back to school, David is more open and comfortable with us holding hands, so we do that a lot. Too much, if you ask me. Before I know it, Christmas break comes around. David asked me on a date to the skating rink. So here I am, getting ready for my date with him. I have no idea what to wear, and half of me doesn't want to go but half does. I have to admit, I do like to skate. I'd rather go with my sister or my friends. They don't ask to hold my hand!

I'm in luck because Teagan gets to come with us since my mom doesn't want me going alone.

"Mar, you've been looking for clothes for fifteen minutes," Teagan says as she stretches across my bed.

"I know. I just don't know what to wear on a real date," I say as I flick through my shirts. "The movies was like a group thing, this is like...the real thing... well, almost..." I turn, smiling at her since she's third-wheeling.

"Can I ask you a question?" She changes position and faces me.

I sigh. "I'd rather you don't, but shoot."

"Why are you dating David if you don't like him?" She sits up, crossing her legs.

I stop rummaging through my clothes.

"Mar, I know you better than anyone," she adds.

"I do like him," I say, moving over to my shoes.

She stands and shuts my door. "Mar, I know you don't."

I try to stay calm. I usually turn red in situations like this. Teagan does know me way too well, so I have to breathe and get through this.

"T, why do you keep saying that?" I ask, picking up a pair of black Vans.

Ugh, Teagan just leave it alone.

"Because my best friend isn't happy," she responds.

I stop what I'm doing and look at her. I feel tears forming in my eyes, but I'm doing everything I can to hold them back.

"I just don't want you dating someone you don't want to date," she says with a slight smile. "But I do want to go skating, so can we still go?"

"T, yes, we are still going. I haven't broken up with David!" I reply with a shocked face.

I mean, Teagan is right even though I don't admit that to her. I don't like David like that. I don't know why I said yes to dating him, exactly. I think I just wanted my classmates to leave me alone about boys and dating, especially Dakota. They're always asking me why I don't have a boyfriend or if I think some guy is cute and I guess saying yes to David was my way to end the interrogations. Actually, it started new ones.

I don't like using David; it's extremely unfair to him since he actually likes me. I would hate to break up with him on a date, but it's the right thing to do, right? Maybe I should wait until it's over.

"Jess texted you," Teagan says, grabbing my phone off the bed. "Wait, you're cool with Jess?" she asks.

I freeze.

I play it cool and respond, "Oh, yeah, we have art together. We're cool." My heart rate increases.

"Oh, cool," she says, tossing my phone over to me.

I catch it. I glance back over to Teagan and she hops back on my bed. I have to stop making situations more than what they are. I'm stressing myself out.

Jess (6:46 p.m.): whatcha doin'?

I glance over at Teagan once more. I know I tend to smile when I'm texting her, so I don't want her to see me. She's reading a J-14 magazine. *Great!*

Me (6:48 p.m.): Getting dressed. Wbu?

Jess (6:48 p.m.): Where ya goin'?

Me (6:49 p.m.): I have my date with David remember?

Jess (6:50 p.m.): oh yeah. Fun! :)

"Are ya'll ready to go?" Mom asks, opening my door.

"Almost. I need to put my clothes on," I reply, grabbing them.

"Hurry up, I'm going to miss the first twenty minutes of *Amazing Race*," she says, pulling the door shut.

My mom is obsessed with that show and *Survivor*. I secretly like them too, but they're old people shows. Mom is thirty-five; is that considered old? Anyway, I leave my room to get dressed in the bathroom. I stare at myself in the mirror.

"You wanna trade places?" I ask mirror me. "No? I didn't think so." I sigh and put on my clothes.

On the way over to the skating rink, I can only think of how and when I'm going to break up with David. I really don't want to hurt his feelings. Do I say the old *It's not you, it's me* line or is that just in movies? Ugh.

As Teagan and I walk into the building, I realize I haven't texted Jess back. I pull my phone out to send a quick text.

Jess (7:17 p.m.): :(

I don't know why, but this text makes me smile. Okay, all of her texts make me smile. Shut-up, I know.

Me (7:34 p.m.): Hey, sorry! I will text you once I leave here.

I place my phone in my pocket and we make our way over to the skates.

"Where's ya boy?" Teagan asks.

I give her a side eye. "Really."

She smiles and asks for her shoe size.

"Hi. I wear a size six but I also can fit a size seven. If you have a six, I would like those better," she says to the worker.

"Really, T?" I frown. "I'm sorry for her," I say to the worker, shaking my head at Teagan still.

This is why she's my best friend. Alongside Jess, of course.

"I'm a seven," I say to the worker.

Teagan and I grab our skates and head for a table. My phone buzzes.

Jess (7:41 p.m.): fine.

Ugh, don't do that.

"What's up, guys? I mean, girls?" David says, walking up.

I place my phone in my pocket.

"Sup, DJ," Teagan says.

I glance at her. "Since when do you—you know what, never mind," I say, shaking my head.

"I'm gonna grab my skates real quick," he says, walking over to the counter.

"At least he smells good," Teagan says, looking back at him.

"Whoa…" I say, frowning.

"I wasn't smelling him like *that*, Mar!" she replies.

"I'd expect that from D, not you," I say to her.

She drops her jaw. "Take it back!"

I pull out my phone. "I'm just saying."

I don't know; that slightly bothered me. Whatever, I guess. I want to sneak in a text to Jess. I can't help it.

Me (7:53 p.m.): don't be a cry baby

I reread our last few texts to go back over our conversation. I usually reread them because they make me happy.

"Hey, Kool-Aid man!" Teagan says, waving her arms.

"Huh, what?" I say suspiciously.

"I see you smiling," she says, giving me an *I'm onto you* look. "Who are you texting?"

My heart picks up the pace. "No, I um—"

Teagan squints her eyes at me. I can't help but laugh, but I'm still kind of annoyed at her for her comment. David's walking back over. "You guys…I mean *girls* ready?" he asks.

"You can call us guys. It doesn't mean you're calling us boys, DJ," Teagan says, bumping her arm into his.

What the hell was that? And what the hell is this "DJ" nonsense? I give her a glare. "We're ready," I say.

Instead of dwelling on thoughts of breaking up with David and Teagan being extremely weird tonight, I decide to just enjoy the evening skating with them. Even though I don't necessarily want to date him doesn't mean we can't be friends, right? Or maybe he'll hate me once I do break up with him. Either way, I wanted to have a fun night, so I try push those thoughts to the back of my head. Teagan won't really leave my head, though; is she flirting with him? In my face? I feel a pang of jealousy.

The question is, why am I jealous? I keep telling myself I don't really like him like that. I mean, David *is* good-looking and very nice. Oh, my head is spinning. I'm so confused.

"I'll catch up!" I yell as I take out my phone. I ignore the messages I have that aren't from Jess.

Jess (7:54 p.m.): I'm not.

Jess (8:03 p.m.): well maybe.

I look around me to make sure Teagan and David are out of sight so I can smile the way I want to. I hate that I love talking to Jess so much. I don't even text Teagan this much.

Me (8:11 p.m.): :) you miss me

I smile and put my phone back in my pocket.

David's messages don't make me smile, but I like getting them. That sounds pretty weird, doesn't it? I mean, I want him to like me. I think I do, anyway. I haven't had very many guys like me, so it's a nice feeling when one does. It makes me feel like I'm not a total loser who can't get a guy. I was going to break up with him, but now, I'm not so sure, especially now with Teagan flirting with him. Should I ask her if she likes him? No, maybe not. Oh, this is crazy. I am so confused. I think I'm a psychopath.

We skate for an hour. Teagan performs a few fake falls so David can help her up.

I think I'm going to hurl all over this place. She is nauseating. Why is she doing this? Oh, why do I keep asking myself this? Ugh, this is so unlike Teagan.

"Want to get some hot chocolate?" David asks as we near the rink exit.

"Sounds good," I say and slip his hand in mine.

Why did I just do that? Oh god. Am I marking my territory? Lord, help me.

We exit the rink, and David heads for the snack bar. He waves me over to help him carry the piping hot cardboard cups filled to the brim.

I hand off one to Teagan, and before I can move, she leans into David and hot chocolate spills on his hand.

"Ouch!" he cries out.

"I'm- I'm so sorry, DJ," she pouts. "I didn't mean to do that. I'm sorry."

DJ? DJ? Did I miss something? Hmm, this does give me a good segue into a breakup. I can be like "You're going to let her flirt with you? I'm done, bye!" But, then again, I don't want to come off as the jealous girlfriend. But… why do I feel like the jealous girlfriend? No, I don't feel like it, I don't know what I feel exactly but I *do* feel like I've missed something between those two. Yikes! I'm going crazy.

We sit and take off our skates. Teagan sits to one side of David, and I'm on the other side. He is definitely the rose between two thorns.

"That was fun," I say as I put on a shoe. "Is your hand okay?"

"It was fun," David replies. "I didn't know you could skate that well, and, yeah, I'll have my mom put something on it when I get home."

"I didn't know either," I say, chuckling.

"Just part of your athletic package," he says, smiling.

Well, don't boost me now, DJ.

Yeah, never say that aloud Marley…

"Thanks," I say, smirking.

David looks around. "So, should we do something else before break ends?" he asks shyly.

Before I can answer, Teagan shouts, "Hell, yeah!"

I guess breaking up isn't on the calendar anytime soon.

"I mean, sure why not," I reply. "Looks like Teagan is all in."

"Cool," he says. "What do you guys…I mean girls want to do?"

"Teagan, why don't you decide," I suggest since she's all gung-ho about it. "Ya know, since you've had so much fun tonight."

Ouch! That came out a little too sarcastically. Oh, well. I guess having her along is better than being alone with DJ. Oh, did I just call him DJ again? I think I need to go home.

"Stop, Mar," she says, side-eyeing me.

I ignore her and grab my cup from the table.

"Well, are you guys ready to ditch this place?" I ask, burning to leave. It's strange and kind of funny how a best friend can be a not-so-best-friend when it comes to guys. I'd expect this flirting from D, but Teagan? I have to admit, I am surprised. And a little mad. And maybe a little jealous. Or maybe it's not jealousy; maybe it's just that I question the motives of my so-called best friend. I know she knows how I feel, but I don't know, has she liked David? Did I unknowingly steal her crush? This is really too much.

Mom told me there'd be days like this. Boys bring out the worst in girls. I never thought I would be a victim of this crap.

So, the whole breakup plan was a bomb, and Teagan clearly wasn't any help. So on to plan B: advice from Jess.

Jess (8:15 p.m.): No.

Me (9:21 p.m.): You do. I need your help.

Jess (9:23 p.m.): Okay, with what?

Me (9:23 p.m.): I want to break up with David… I think.

Jess (9:24 p.m.): :O

Jess (9:24 p.m.): aren't you on a date with him??

Me (9:25 p.m.): Home now. I want to get it over with

Jess (9:25 p.m.): Idk!! Um.

Me (9:26 p.m.): You're no help.

Jess (9:26 p.m.): I'm sorry:(

Jess (9:27 p.m.): Do you not like him anymore?

Too many questions for me to think about right now plus, I want to complain about Teagan, but I don't have the energy. I plop onto my bed and pull up the covers. I feel a little chilled. It's probably from being at the rink; it might as well had been snowing in there.

My phone dings. I look. It's David.

David (10:01 p.m.): I had a nice time tonight. Thanks for coming :)

Why does he have to be so nice? It's not helping me to break up with him. I answer Jess.

Me (10:13 p.m.): I don't know.

I answer David.

Me (10:14 p.m.): Me too. Night.

It's been a long evening. I turn off my phone and roll over, shivering.

Chapter 7

It's the last Saturday before break ends. I am cold and tired. I get up to grab a pair of fuzzy socks; they're known for keeping my toesies warm. My drawers squeak. I hate them so much. I need new ones. I slip my socks on, but they aren't warming me up quick enough, so I decide to lay in bed until I warm up. I barely have a chance to close my eyes again when Mom knocks.

"Baby, you okay? Can I come in?"

Did I mention that I loathe when she calls me *baby*? She must have heard my drawer. Mom takes the first ticket available when she hears Kendal or me awake in the mornings.

"Yeah," I answer.

She walks over to me and her hand falls to my head. "You're burning up. Where don't you feel good? Does your stomach hurt?"

Here we go...

"I'm okay. I just feel tired and cold."

"Get some rest, and I'll check on you later."

I nod and close my eyes. I feel like crap. I sneeze; it hurts and my nose runs. I grab a tissue and my phone. I turn it on. Nothing.

Wow, nothing? This has to be a morning first. Wait. What time is it? I glance at the clock on my nightstand. Oh, it's 8 a.m. No wonder no one has texted me. Who's up at eight on a Saturday? Only me…and Mom.

I sleep most of the day, and when I finally wake, I have twenty messages waiting for me. Holy cow! This is the fame I strive for.

Just kidding.

I open each one and read. David. Teagan. Dakota. David again. Teagan again. Dakota again. Wash, rinse, repeat.

No Jess. Ouch.

I toss my phone to the side of the bed and slowly lower my feet to the floor. I need to pee. I need water, too. My mouth is dry. I don't feel chilled anymore, so that's a good thing, right?

Mom hears me in the bathroom with her bat ears. She calls up to me from the stairway. "Mar, David has called a few times. You can call him when you feel up to it."

"You told him I'm sick?" I call down to her.

"Um, yes. Wasn't I supposed to?"

I hear a slight pout in her voice. "No, Mom. That's fine," I tell her and wobble back to my room.

I sit on the edge of my bed, fighting the urge to lay down. Hopefully now that Mom knows I'm awake, she'll bring me soup and water or Ginger Ale or something—anything at this point. I can hear ice cubes clanking in a glass, and I know it won't be long.

And it isn't. Mom comes in the room with a tray table I'm sure she found in the garage.

"You are really dramatic," I say with a slight smile as I reach for the water. "I can't eat all this."

"Eat what you can," she says, leaving the room.

I take some water and a few spoonful's of soup. I eye some grapes and decide against them. I feel a bit better, so I text David since he was nice enough to check on me and blow up my phone with messages.

Me (3:40 p.m.): Hey. I feel a little bit better. Slept most of the day

David (3:41 p.m.): I was worried about you. You okay?

Me (3:42 p.m.): Ya. I'm good

David (3:43 p.m.): Not sure if Teagan messaged you. Going rollerblading tonight. That's what she picked. You probably not going?

What? I'm probably not going? I'm sick in bed. What does he think and why does it sound like they're going anyway, without me? I text Teagan.

Me (3:45 p.m.): Sup?

Teagan (3:47 p.m.): Hey, Mar! Tryin to decide what to wear tonight

Me (3:48 p.m.): Wear? You going on a date??

Silence.

More silence.

Even more silence.

Me (4:00 p.m.): ????

Nothing.

What the hell. Teagan is notorious for texting back instantly; she's usually glued to her phone. And why would they go skating without me?

I decide not to wait for a text, and I dial her number. My voice barely works, but I want to know what's going on.

"Hey," she answers.

"You didn't text me back," I say. "What's going on, best friend?"

"I, um…"

"You um what?"

"I didn't know you were sick, and, well, we made plans to go to the skating rink. We didn't know you were sick and figured you'd be going."

"So why didn't you cancel?"

"I- I guess I don't know why. I will, though."

"You will? Why? Because I called you? Because you're going out with *my* boyfriend?"

I didn't just say that, did I? Oh, the green monster is inside of me. No wonder I'm sick.

"What's the big deal?" she asks. "You don't like him. You told me so. And, well…"

"Well, what?" I say, my voice getting a little louder.

"Well, I'm going to cancel. We can't go without you. I was only trying to help you. Honest."

"Help me what?"

"Ditch him," she says. "You said you wanted to break up with him, so I was only trying to make it easier for both of you."

"Easier how? So he ends up liking you next? You're not making sense, so go. Have a good time. Kiss him, for goodness' sake. I don't care. I'm going back to bed."

I end the call, and a tear falls to my cheek. What's going on? What's wrong with me? Why do I feel like the world is caving in on me? I feel betrayed by David and Teagan. Teagan, mostly, I think David is genuinely clueless in the situation, but Teagan knows what she's doing. That really bothers me. Why would they still make plans if they didn't hear from me all day?

I send David a text.

Me (4:20 p.m.): Have fun skating with my best friend

I slam my phone shut and turn it off. I think of turning it back on to text Jess, but she's probably sick of hearing my "woe is me" these past few days. Plus, she hasn't texted me today. I'm not really in the mood to talk with anyone, anyway.

I hear the house phone ring. I'm sure it's David. I yell down to Mom that if it's for me, I'm not taking any calls for the rest of the day.

There's a part of me that wants to talk to her, to ask her about the best friend jealousy thing. Mom is good with that kind of stuff. I want to know if Teagan broke the girl code or if she truly believes she's doing me a favor. She sure put on a show if she was only acting.

I guess for now, I'll shut down my mind and not think about David or Teagan...or Jess. New for me, I know. I need a break from all of it. Life was so much simpler when I was in fifth grade when my biggest concerns were beating Tyler in Mario Kart. Bragging rights were very dangerous in our neighborhood. Oh, happier times, how I miss thee.

I hear Mom's footsteps coming up the stairs. I hug Mr. Slam Dunk. Hey, I'm not too old to have a stuffed bear. Plus, he is wearing a cute little Sharks basketball uniform.

"Come in," I say before she knocks.

"Mar, David called again. He said he hopes you feel better and he'll call you tomorrow, but if you feel up to talking, he'll be home all night."

Oh. The they must have called off their date. Well, well, well

"Thanks, Mom. I think I'll not take any calls tomorrow either. I need some 'me' time."

"Is everything okay?" she asks with concern.

This is where I want to scream, "No, it isn't!" and break down and sob on her shoulder as she rubs my back. This is when I want Mom to be Mommy, and me to be little again. Instead, I lie and say that everything is fine, I'm just a little worn out.

She tiptoes out of my room as if I'm asleep, and I smile. I guess sometimes all I need is to know my mom's wisdom is just a few steps away.

I wish I knew how the conversation went with David and Teagan. I didn't even know they had each other's numbers. My head hurts; I'm done thinking about it for the weekend.

The skating rink? One, we just went ice skating last night, but of course, Teagan would come up with something where she could show off those falls again. Ugh.

Brain…go to sleep.

Chapter 8

No one was happier to walk through the school entrance doors than me. Break is over, and what started as fun didn't quite end that way. We have to make up a snow day today, so the new semester begins tomorrow. Weird, I know.

It's been three days since I've had any contact with anyone. I am starting to like my new life as a loner...kinda. I really only missed Jess.

For three days and three nights, my phone never stopped. There were so many text messages from David and Jess and Teagan and Dakota. In some ways, I feel bad for ignoring everyone, but in other ways, I needed to. Too much drama for this girl!

I hear footsteps behind me, then a tap on my shoulder.

"Hey, Mar. Where the hell have you been? I've been calling and texting and worried sick about you."

"I'm fine, T," I say and dart ahead of her.

"Hey, wait up," she calls out, but I keep moving.

Oh, boy. Here comes David. I see him heading in my direction. Quick, Marley. Think. I look around. I've seen a character in my video game jump in a trash bin, but I'll be taking a hard pass on that. Ugh, I have nowhere to hide, and he's approaching with lightning speed.

"Hey, why haven't you called me back or answered my messages? I've been worried about you," he says.

"I'm good. I just needed some space."

"Does that mean that you're dumping me?" he asks, a boyish look crossing his face. "I—"

"No, it doesn't mean that."

What did I just do? I had my chance and blew it. Oh, well, maybe I'm not ready to send him off into the arms of Teagan. I feel so betrayed by them both. Why would they even think of hanging out without me? They aren't even friends! My feelings and my ego are crushed.

David looks at me, perplexed. "Can I walk you to class?"

"Sure," I say and give him a slight smile. I don't want him getting overly excited, thinking that we're a happy couple.

"Did you have fun skating with Teagan?" I ask, pretending that I didn't get his message.

"No, we didn't go. I didn't want to go without you," he says and takes my hand and squeezes it.

I wish Teagan would see this. Oh god, but I hope Jess doesn't. Oh, what a competition I'm having with myself and my friends. It's wrong, and I don't know why I feel this way. My sister says it's normal junior high stuff, and I'll grow out of it.

I sure hope I do and soon.

David drops me off at my first-period class. He gives me puppy eyes as if we're never going to see each other again. In some ways, I wish we weren't.

I walk into class and take my seat. I'm prepared for forty minutes of daydreaming. I have no desire to pay attention to my teacher, who, by the way, in case I didn't mention, has the worst comb-over I've ever seen. Seriously, embrace your baldness, Mr. Turner. He has so much hair gel on his head it kind of tilts to one side.

Ugh, don't be mean cause you're in a mood, Marley.

Sorry, Mr. Turner.

I wonder what Jess is thinking. She probably thinks I'm mad or maybe that my phone is broken. She does know I throw it a lot in fits of rage. Hopefully, that's all she thinks. I wish I hadn't ignored her. I hate that I did, but I truly needed the alone time.

Did I mention that I hate being twelve?

And to make things worse, I started the monthly. So, thrust me into a more confusing world of pads versus tampons, as if I didn't already have enough confusion in my life. And it's so gross. Whoever decided that girls needed this in their lives had to be on drugs. Cramps and headaches and grumpiness...yeah, who decided to grace girls with this honor? I'll gladly return it.

So apparently, I am now officially a "woman," so my mom tells me. That means I can reproduce, as if the world needs more of me. Mom gave me the "talk" about the birds and the bees. I won't get into details because she sure didn't. Thank goodness for health class, which I have next and might actually pay attention to.

Well, the pad/tampon debate was settled by Mom. She said I could get sick from tampons. She read in the news it's happened to others, so I get the bulky pad that probably shows for all the world to see. I've yet to figure out how I'll play basketball with a half-diaper thing stuck to my undies.

"Marley...Marley...I'm talking to you. Perhaps paying attention would behoove you," Mr. Turner says, snapping me out of my sanitary napkin thoughts.

"Huh? I'm sorry; what?" The class laughs. "Yes, I said I'm going to call your mother and tell her you don't pay attention in class," he says with a bit of anger.

Okay, have fun with that, Stanley. Stanley is Mr. Turner's first name. Anyway, Mom isn't a big fan of Mr. Turner. She had to call him for mistakenly giving me a bad grade on a homework assignment. He claimed the grade he entered was correct, but my paper said otherwise. He told Mom I must have changed the grade, which I didn't. I don't have old man handwriting. So, yeah, not really worried about him calling. She's not going to care that much. Hopefully.

The bell rings, and I am saved from the wrath of Stanley.

I'm no more than out the door when David runs up to me. Good grief. How did he get here so fast?

"Geez, what the heck? I say, frowning at him.

"Walking you to class. I left my class a few minutes early."

I look at him. "Don't you think that's kind of weird? Leaving class to walk me to mine?"

"No," he says nonchalantly.

Yippee, now I have a suffocating boyfriend I don't even know if I like and a best friend who isn't acting like a best friend, and a secret friend I like more than my boyfriend and best friend, and then there's Dakota, who can be so annoying but probably wouldn't be doing the fake damsel-in-distress falling in front of the boyfriend I don't know if I like, or maybe she would. Who knows at this point? Maybe everyone wants David. Am I dating the Zac Efron of the school?

Well, that pretty much sums up my life concisely. I seem to have these trapped emotions that I can't let escape, or they won't escape. I don't know which it is, but the turmoil that my insides are going through gets to me sometimes. Okay, all of the time.

The adults call these the awkward years and the "coming of age" years. I just want to know who I am and where I fit into this world. Heck, I don't even know where I fit in this school anymore.

David says goodbye as he heads to his next class, and I walk into health. Hopefully, he won't be waiting for me when class ends.

Teagan walks in and she strolls past me, dropping something on my desk. It looks like a note, so I brush it aside and pretend I'm not interested. Besides, I don't need to be caught reading a note in class. That's good for lunch detention, or worse, the teacher will confiscate it and read it out loud. Which I sure as hell don't need in my life.

I listen carefully as my teacher discusses the digestive system. Oh, it's so much fun to look at slides of guts before lunch.

Brandon yells out something about it being the path of a fart, and the class laughs. I don't. It seems so immature, but that's half of the boys in this school. Plus, the joke was funny in like third grade. His mind clearly never left grade school. David oddly doesn't act like that. He acts his age, and sometimes, even older.

I am dreading art. I wonder what Jess will say or do. Maybe she's forgotten who I am. Some days, I wish I could forget who I am...if I only knew who I am. Ha! My mom would say I'll discover my true self soon enough, but for now I should enjoy being a confused, restless preteen. I guess there's a magic wand that transforms all preteens on their thirteenth birthday. I look forward to the transformation, but for now...

I'll try to reinvent the sanitary napkin.

Chapter 9

I'm excited to be home early. Coach Leslie called off practice today. I'm actually glad because today was a bit much and I didn't want to be in practice with Teagan. Jess wasn't in class today, so I'm assuming she wasn't at school. I wouldn't know because we haven't talked in a few days. I don't like that at all. I turn on my TV and lay in my bed. I pull out my phone to text her.

Me (4:29 p.m.): Hiya

As I wait for Jess to respond, I go to let Mom know Mr. Turner might be calling her unless he was bluffing. He was being quite dramatic, if you ask me. She isn't mad at me, so that's good news. I make my way back to my room. I honestly just want to chill the rest of the night.

Jess (4:36 p.m.): Hmm

It feels nice to talk to this kid again.

Me (4:37 p.m.): Don't hate me

Jess (4:37 p.m.): Hmmmmm

Is it weird that I enjoy this? I smile and reply.

Me (4:38 p.m.): I'm a terrible friend, I know

Jess (4:38 p.m.): Mhmm

Me (4:39 p.m.): How long are you gonna do this?

Jess (4:39 p.m.): How many days did you not text me?

Touché, Jess. Touché.

Me (4:40 p.m.): I've been overwhelmed. I'm sorry.

Jess (4:41 p.m.): You're supposed to be able to talk to me :(

Me (4:41 p.m.): I know I just... I don't know.

Jess (4:42 p.m.): I can call you. I'm home sick.

Jess and I have oddly never talked on the phone before. This makes me nervous.

Me (4:43 p.m.): Okay, sure.

I sit up in my bed. I buff my pillows and straighten up my comforter. What am I doing? Jess can't see me or my room. I'm going crazy.

My phone buzzes. It's David.

David (4:46 p.m.): Hey :)

I really need to pull the plug. I really need to talk to Teagan. I ignore his message.

My phone rings and I stare at it. Jess's name is scrolling across, and it makes my heart skip a beat. I pick up.

"Hello?"

"Hey, stranger."

I smile. "Hey."

"So, talk to me," she says.

I tell Jess what happened. She doesn't take any sides in the Teagan situation. She thinks I should talk to her. Which I agree. She was pretty short and dry with the David situation...I don't think she likes him very much. She expressed a few times during the call how she's still mad at me so I will have to spend the next week making it up to her. I don't mind, though.

Once we hang up, I dial Teagan. "Hey, Mar," Teagan says.

"You don't have 'Mar' privileges right now," I say.

Silence.

I'm trying to figure out how to go about this. It's a really annoying and confusing situation. "Do you like David?" I ask. I couldn't wait any longer.

Silence.

"I don't know, Mar...Marley."

I don't exactly know what to say. "Oh," is all my brain lets me say.

"I don't know what to say, Mar. I knew you didn't like him like that."

"Marley," I say.

Am I being a baby? Once again, she's right. *Ugh. I really hate this.* If she does like him, which it seems she does, I just don't like the way she went about it. We could have talked about it instead of her keeping it a secret from me. She could have waited until I ended it with him, like, there were so many other options rather than flirting with him in my face and setting up a date while I was on my deathbed. But she's right. How can I be so territorial with someone I supposedly don't want? I think I'm ready to retire the seventh grade.

I'm tempted to call in to one of those radio hotlines where people tell the radio host their sad life story and get callers to weigh in on their life.

Teagan has been my right-hand girl for the past year and a half; she's never betrayed me before. I want to give her another chance. I think if it were Dakota, I'd kick her to the curb.

I hear sniffing in the background. "T, are you crying?" I ask.

"No," she sniffs.

"I can hear you," I say.

"No, you can't."

"You like him, don't you?" I ask again.

"I really don't know, Mar...ley."

I roll my eyes. "You can call me Mar."

"Why didn't you tell me you liked him? Instead, you flirted with him in front of me," I say, lying down.

"I thought if I could get him to like me, then it would make your situation easier. I went too far. Mar, you mean more to me than David."

"I know I'm not being fair," I say. I mean come on, I'm not...and now that I'm a woman, I can admit that. "If you like him, fine. I think I grew to like him. He's really nice and sweet, but no, my head isn't in the relationship."

"I don't want a relationship with him."

"Well, whatever you want with him," I say.

"After I realized how hurt you were, I told myself I won't do it."

This really is a mess and in true Marley fashion, I'm to blame. I created this mess. I said yes to dating a guy I didn't know. I told Teagan I didn't like him. I did this.

I'm getting another call. It's Jess again.

"I'll call you back."

"Okay."

Ugh, Teagan sounds pitiful. I don't know if I feel bad for being so harsh or if I gave her the treatment she deserved.

"Wrong number?" I answer.

"Shut up."

I laugh. "What's up?"

Talking to Jess makes me care less and less about the situation I've been throwing a fit over for the past few days. I don't know. She makes me forget about the world.

"I'm sick. I want to talk."

"Marley Waters reporting for duty."

She laughs and then coughs. "Don't make me laugh. It hurts."

"Jess, I'm a comedian," I say.

"Oh, really? Since when?"

"Shut up; you already knew," I reply.

Jess and I stay on the phone until I have to get off for dinner. I eat dinner as fast as I can, scaring Mom. She thinks I have a tapeworm. I just want to finish quickly so I can call Jess back.

I think of calling Teagan again, but I figure it's best to let that simmer for a while. I'm not sure what happened to her liking Sam—maybe it's because Jess is dating him, but she sure switched gears fast.

Whoever said junior high would be fun didn't live a life like mine.

Chapter 10

Finally, a new semester. New semesters mean new classes! This is so weird considering last semester was yesterday. Anyway, the downside is I have zero classes with Jess, including electives. The schedule gods hate me, clearly. The upside is that we have the same lunch hour, but our group of friends differs, so we most likely won't be eating lunch together. *Ugh.* My first class doesn't start for fifteen minutes, so I head to my locker.

Teagan and I resolved our issues, or should I say issue. We had a really long talk on the on the phone last night. We agreed that we won't let anyone, especially a boy, come between us again. She's been eyeing Dante Jennings lately; he plays on the football team and he isn't that cute to me, but that's good ol' Teagan, on to the next.

"Marley, Mar!" Ahh, déjà vu to the first day of school. I know who that was. I turn around to see Teagan smiling like she'd just won the lottery. I run to her and give her a hug.

Our new lockers are ready today as well so I'm curious to see if I don't have to shove my backpack inside anymore.

"Oh my gosh, dude. I'm so happy to see you right now. What locker are you?" I ask, praying hers is near mine.

Unfolding her letter from the mail, she says, "I have 2671. What about you?!"

The locker gods are on my side. "I'm 2673!" I exclaim.

"Yes!" we yell simultaneously. Our lockers are right next to each other, and I couldn't be happier.

We skip over to check out who else is in our neck of the woods. On our way, I can't help but scan the halls for Jess. I don't see her. We make it to the hall of our lockers and it looks like a party is happening. All of our friends are over here. I say my *Hey*s and give my hugs and make my way to my locker, leaving Teagan because she likes to talk. I try my combination, and I know I will have a hard time as I usually do. To my defense, it's been three weeks since I had to use one of these.

"Struggling?" I hear as I'm physically abusing the lock. I haven't heard this voice in five long days. My anger turns into a soft smile.

It's Jess. She got a haircut—well, more like a trim, but it's nice. I can say that, right? I laugh and reply, "Nope, not at all." I'm lying, obviously; this piece-of-crap lock was giving me the blues. So much for being brand new.

"Mmm, sure…okay," she says, grinning as she takes off her backpack. She starts to unlock the locker next to mine.

"No way this is your locker," I say, looking at her like she's full of it.

Looking over at me, she responds, *"Nope, not at all."* She smiles as she continues trying the lock.

It opens.

I smile and keep trying mine. What are the odds of her locker being next to mine and why can I never open a damn locker? Nevertheless, thank you, locker gods.

She grabs a few supplies and puts her backpack inside.

"See ya later, gator," she says, giving my arm a light squeeze. "You sure you don't need help?"

Smiling—because when the hell am I not around her—I say, "This locker won't defeat me."

She laughs and walks away to her first class.

I wish I could explain how I feel about Jess in a way that would make sense. The thing is, I can't. I don't know why, but I have this soft spot for her. It's not like I like her like *that*. Plus, that's weird, right? Liking your best friend who's a *girl*?

The morning goes by fairly quickly. I was really nerding out on my classes, which took my mind off of Jess and David. I'm still trying to break up with him, eight years later. Besides that, I'm really excited for our last basketball game tonight.

Lunch is interesting. Both teams can fit in the new cafeteria now. This constitutes an important day; it's like the first day of school all over again. This is where you establish where you and your posse will be sitting until the last day of school. Choose wisely.

I wait up for Teagan and Dakota before I get into the lunch line.

"T, Dakota! Over here!" I holler through a group of classmates, waving my arms like a psycho.

They push their way through and we make our way inside.

"Holy shit, this place is huge," Teagan says, shoving papers in a binder.

Staring as she wrinkles her homework, I say, "I know. Where are we even going to sit?"

"Let's get that table by the window before someone else does!" Dakota suggests and runs across the cafeteria.

"Cool with me," I say, following.

We set up shop at our new table and go to hop in the lunch line. Of course, I find myself scanning the room for a certain someone, but I can't make it obvious. I'm also doing everything I can to avoid David. After we pay, we join the rest of our friends at our table. We start chatting, talking about tonight's game. I feel my phone buzz, but I take a few minutes to take it out.

Jess (11:18 am): hey...

I try so hard not to smile. Remember, anything I do will be held against me. Self-control is in full go-mode right now.

Me (11:22 am): hey stranger. You in the cafe?

Jess (11:24 am): yes. I'm next to your table

Oh god, I might be sick. Don't look. Wait, but if I don't look, won't that be worse? That will definitely make me look suspicious. Ugh, this is exhausting, what is wrong with me?

I get myself together in a span of ten seconds and look over to the table next to us. One hundred percent wrong table—it's a bunch of guys doing only god knows what. So my only other choice is to look the other way. I muscle up the strength to turn my neck 180 degrees to the left. Jess is on the far side of the table. She smiles and looks back down to her phone. I do the same.

Me (11:25 am): you stalking me jess??

Jess (11:25 am): hahah shutup Marley.

Me (11:26 am): just saying, kidnapping is very real

Jess (11:26 am): hahaha

Me (11:26 am): what was on your lunch menu, home school

Jess doesn't eat school lunches. She brings her lunch from home.

Jess (11:27 am): haha oh you're funny today I see

Me (11:27a m): lol I'm always funny.

Jess (11:28 am): sometimes… turkey sandwich

Me (11:29 am): don't hate me cause you aint me…yum.

I know, I'm corny. Shut up.

Jess (11:30 am): hahaa you're ridiculous

Before I can respond, my friend Katrina is yelling my name. "Helloooooo, earth to Marleyyy," she drags.

I look up as if I'm guilty of a crime. "Yep?" I say, like I'm guilty of said crime.

Inching her body over the table, she says with a devilish smile, "So who are we texting?"

My body starts to overheat per usual. "Huh?" I respond.

Dakota nudges me. "Yeah, you're all smiling and whatnot." She raises an eyebrow at me.

Dear god, if you love me, get me out of this.

Chuckling, I respond, "No one. I was just reading something." I place my phone in my pocket.

Teagan glances at me like she can see through my lies.

"Mmhm," Dakota says, biting into her burger.

"We're watching you, Marley. I know it's a boy! Is it David?" Katrina says with excitement.

"No, it's not David. I was reading something on MySpace!" I make up.

She sits back down in her seat. "Okay, okay, if you say so."

Oh my god. That was almost disastrous. I mean, I could've just said I was texting my friend Jess, but they would've asked why I was smiling like that when it was only her. Moral of the story: I need to control my face. We finish eating and chat for what feels like three minutes before the bell rings.

Lunch is over. *Boo.* I have two more classes for the day. Luckily, we get to stay after school until our game. I spend the day wondering if Jess will be able to make it. I know she has tennis every day, so she most likely won't. It's probably better that way so I don't have to play under pressure, especially with this being a huge game to win our conference. Honestly, I think I would throw up if Jess actually did come to my games.

After my seventh hour, which is our last class of the day, I make my way to my locker to grab my basketball bag. When I get there, Jess is at her locker with Dani. I walk up to my locker without speaking to them. Sometimes, I feel like it's best if I don't speak to Jess when she's around people so they don't see me fawning over her.

"Oh, really?" Jess says, opening my locker door wider.

"What happened?" I say with a fake confused face, smiling.

Jess shakes her head and closes her locker. "See you tomorrow," she says, bumping into me.

I laugh to myself and continue putting away my books. Jess isn't actually mad at me, or at least I don't think she is. I glance down the hall at her.

She's definitely the coolest kid in this school...

"Mar, you ready?" Teagan asks, walking up to me.

"Yeah, are we just going to chill in the gym?" I ask.

Teagan starts stuffing more papers into her backpack. "No, I think we're going to chill in Coach Leslie's classroom."

"Do you need a binder, T? I'm concerned at this point," I ask, pointing at her mess of a backpack.

"Shut up, Mar!" she replies, laughing.

"Hey, you got it." I laugh, shutting my locker. "Where's Dakota?"

"I don't know. I haven't seen her since lunch," she responds.

"She'll meet us in the classroom," I say, putting on my backpack. We take off walking.

"Hey, Marley," I hear behind me.

Teagan and I look at each other.

I turn around. "Hey, David." I walk over to him. Teagan is hesitant to come over, I'm assuming because of the whole ordeal we had. I've made up my mind. I'm fine, really.

"Good luck tonight," he says, handing me a Snickers bar. "I hear these are good for energy."

I take it. "Thanks. Good luck to you, too."

"Oh, we're going to lose; you guys actually have a chance," he says, shrugging.

"Yeah, you guys are pretty bad," I say, smirking.

"Hey, I can't do all of the work by myself."

"Yes, that's what's happening," I say sarcastically.

David smiles. I think he thinks I'm flirting. I'm so exhausted from this roller coaster of a relationship, I'm just being friendly. I don't even feel like I'm dating him anymore. I just need the right time break it to him without hurting him. I'm not heartless.

"Hey, T," he says, looking behind me.

This makes everything awkward again.

"Hey," Teagan says.

I haven't figured out if David is just really nice and friendly or he's one of those smooth-talking boys who charm their way to get girls. He seems genuine, but who knows.

"Well, we have to get to our coach's classroom," I say.

"Oh, yeah. Well, good luck. I'll be cheering for you," he says, opening his arms for a hug.

"Oh, um, okay," I say awkwardly, leaning in for the hug.

"I'll be your good luck charm," he says, smiling, walking away backward.

Oh, wow. Okay… um… well… probably not.

He really never gives me a window to break it off. He's always so nice, which makes my life so much harder. It's settled. I'm stuck in this relationship for the rest of my life. Sound the wedding bells.

Teagan and I make our way to the classroom. I go straight for Coach Leslie's beanbag chair.

"Ahh," I say, sinking my body into the beanbag. "This is nice."

The classroom door swings open. "What the heck!" Dakota yells as she enters the classroom.

Peace is often taken for granted.

"Y'all left me!" she yells, slamming her bag on a desk.

"D, it's not that serious," Teagan says as she plays on the dry erase board.

Our other teammates don't really get involved when anger is amidst us.

I continue to lay there.

"Marley, do you hear me?" she yells.

"Yes; yes, I do," I say with my eyes closed.

Dakota goes on yelling about us leaving her for the next ten minutes. When Coach Leslie makes it back, she tells her to chill. God bless.

We have about an hour to burn before we can head to the gym. Our parent club is in the gym setting up for the last game. A lot of our classmates will be at this game, so I'm getting more and more nervous as time goes by. I know once I hit the court, my nerves will go away, but it's just the game day jitters. I figure I'll check in on Jess to see if she's actually mad at me.

Me (4:03 p.m.): Hey.

Jess (4:04 p.m.): No

Me (4:04 p.m.): What I do?

Jess (4:05 p.m.): being mean.

Maybe she is upset. Crap.

Me (4:05 p.m.): Me?

Jess (4:06 p.m.): yes.

Me (4:07 p.m.): I wasn't trying to be. I'm sorry.

She takes a few minutes to respond, so, of course, in my mind I feel like our friendship is over.

Jess (4:13 p.m.): mhm.

"Mar, want some M&Ms?" Teagan asks me, shoving like ten in her mouth.

I look up and frown. "What? Ew, no, Teagan!" I go back to texting.

Me (4:15 p.m.): I am. :(

Jess (4:16 p.m.): Better be. See you tonight.

Wait, what?! Is she coming? Okay, I know I wanted her to come but, please, God, no.

Me (4:16 p.m.): Tonight???

Jess (4:17 p.m.): oops I meant tomorrow. :)

I actually don't know if that makes me sad or happy. I think sad because every chance to see or hang with Jess, I take.

Me (4:18p.m.): Haha I figured. Wait, you're done texting me until tomorrow?!

Jess (4:19 p.m.): Oh wait, huh?

Me (4:20 p.m.): What?????

Jess (4:21 p.m.): Idk hahaha

"Ladies, let's get ready to make our way to the gym," Coach Leslie announces.

Me (4:22 p.m.): Smh. I gtg. Talk to you who knows when!

Jess (4:23 p.m.): :)

Jess actually just made my head hurt, but I'm not mad about it.

The team and I get our things together and make our way to the gym. On the way over, our classmates are outside cheering us on. I feel like Kobe Bryant, to be honest with you. When we get inside the foyer, Coach Leslie asks us to go straight to the locker room. We change into our uniforms and wait for our cue to come out. It feels like hours. I think since I'm so anxious, time feels as if it's moving in slow motion.

Coach Leslie comes inside the locker room. "Okay, ladies, let's leave it all on the court tonight!" she yells.

The team cheers.

"D, take it away!" I yell.

"On three!" she screams.

"One. Two. Three…Sharks!" We scream and cheer.

We run out of the locker room toward the gym. "Boom Boom Pow" by the Black Eyed Peas begins playing.

We all give each other "the look" and take off running to
the court, tearing through a custom-made banner that reads
"Undefeated!"

Well, we better not lose this game.

The crowd is insane. Our games haven't been this packed
all year; it's like the entire town is here. We run to the middle
of the court and wave to everyone in the bleachers.

"Layup lines, let's go!" I yell over the music.

The energy in the building is amazing. We are playing
Meddington Junior High, who are also undefeated. This
game is gonna be crazy. I felt good in warmups. I was hitting
my jumpers and finishing my layups strong. I'm ready.

The clock buzzes to signal the game getting ready start.
We jog over to the huddle to prep.

"Okay, ladies, this is our game, we just have to focus!"
Coach Leslie yells over the music.

"We got this, y'all; don't worry about the talk. Let's just
play!" I say, placing my hand in the middle. "D, take it away!"

"I Gotta Feeling" by the Black Eyed Peas begins playing.

We all look up at the stereos. We look back at each other,
smiling.

I nod to Dakota to take it away. "On three!" she yells.

"On three," I repeat.

"One…Two…Three…Sharks!" We yell and throw our
hands in the air.

Starting five take to the court. We circle around for jump
ball. I'm vibing to the song and doing last-second stretches.

"*That tonight's gonna be a good night,*" I sing to myself,
bobbing my head.

As I stretch my right arm, I glance over to the student
section. I see the only person I would want to see sitting

front row holding a poster with my number on it. I can't do anything but smile. Each girl on the tennis team has a poster with a number on it. Jess has mine.

The ref blows the whistle and throws the ball in the air for the tip-off.

We get the tip and I run down the court. Dakota throws me the ball and I dribble in for the layup. The defense collapses in on me, so I dish it to Teagan. She shoots it off the backboard for the score.

The crowd roars.

"Yes, T!" I yell and fist-pump. My nerves go away and now it's game time.

As the game goes on, the score goes back and forth. Coach Leslie barely gives me and Dakota breaks.

We're sitting at a tie at halftime. In the locker room, Coach Leslie tells us to keep playing with heart and hunger. We hype each other up and go back out for the second half. I glance at Jess for a quick second on the way out. She waves and holds up the sign with my number on it. I take a playful bow and run over to the huddle.

The second half starts and we continue back-and-forth play, trading buckets each trip down the court...

There are twenty-seven seconds left in the fourth quarter and the game is tied 47 to 47. Dakota fouls out, which is huge because she's one of our main scorers. I have to channel in my inner Kobe and clutch the win.

Sara takes the ball out and passes it to me. I dribble down the floor and get ready to pass the ball to Alex. The defender runs into me, causing a loose ball. The ref doesn't call a foul.

"Foul, ref!" Coach Leslie yells from the bench.

The crowd begins booing.

They run for the ball, pick it up, and dribble toward the goal.

I look up at the clock; there are eleven seconds left. I get up and sprint down the court. As I chase the girl with the ball, the crowd is roaring. She goes up for the layup…

I jump as high and far as I can to block the shot. I feel my fingers tip the ball as I bump her body.

The ref blows the whistle for the foul.

I knew I fouled, but I had no choice. I throw my hands on my head and look up at the clock. It's still 47 to 47, but now with four seconds left in the game. They have two free throws.

Having fouled out, I make my way over to the bench. The crowd cheers my name.

With Dakota and me both fouling out, it definitely makes it harder on us. We're the playmakers on the team.

Coach Leslie calls a time-out. "Okay, listen; we aren't out of this," she starts as she pulls out her clipboard.

She draws up a play for Sara, Teagan, and Alex. "T, make sure you are here as soon as the shot comes off the rim," she says, pointing to the board. "You have to throw the ball like a baseball so we have enough time for the shot. Alex, be ready. You guys can do this!" she says, yelling over the crowd.

"D, take it away!" I yell.

"On three!" Dakota yells as loud as she can.

"One. Two. Three…Sharks!" the crowd yells with us.

It startles us, and we all smile from ear to ear, looking into the stands.

"We can do this," I whisper to myself. My entire body is shaking.

"Come on, T!" I yell, giving her two thumbs up.

The crowd falls silent as both teams line up for the free throws.

She takes three dribbles and shoots the ball…

Swish.

The opponents section cheers loudly, stomping their feet on the bleachers.

I'm shaking so much, I am shaking the bench. I'm so nervous, but I have to be the leader my teammates expect me to be.

I stand. "Alex! Brie!" I yell, waving them over.

They look over at me and get as close as they can.

"Alex, as soon as the ball leaves her hands, run down the court on this side and cut hard and fast to the other side three-point line," I start. "Brie, run with Alex and on her cut, set a hard and sturdy screen on her defender. You *cannot* move; they're calling everything on us."

They look at each other in confidence and shake their heads, confirming they understand.

"Oh, and Alex," I say. She turns around. "Let T know where the shot is coming from." I give her a fist bump. "Breathe and let it fly." I nod.

Coach Leslie comes over to me. "That's how you become a leader," she says, smiling at me and patting me on the back.

I smile at her.

Back to the game.

The ref gives the opponent the ball. She takes her three dribbles. The gym is so quiet you can hear a pin drop. She lets it fly…

The ball bounces off the rim!

Sara smacks the ball back, and Teagan catches it. Alex simultaneously runs up the court and cuts off of Brie's screen to the opposite three-point line.

"Alex!" Teagan yells as loud as she can.

She throws the ball like a baseball...

I stand to see what the hell is about to happen.

Alex catches it and pulls up for the three...

As she lets the ball go out of her hands, Dakota grabs my wrist, damn near breaking it...

The clock buzzes as the ball is halfway in the air...

SWISH!

"Oh my God!" I scream, sprinting to Alex.

The crowd goes insane.

As we storm the court, the student section follows. "Party in the USA" by Miley Cyrus starts playing over the PA system. Everyone begins to dance and sing.

"I hopped off the plane at LAX with a dream and my cardigan!" we sing.

"Your Lady Sharks are officially undefeated, ladies and gentlemen!" Principal Miller yells into the mic.

"Woo!" we yell with the crowd.

"Hell, yeah!" I say, grabbing and hugging Teagan. "I told you, you had it!"

"Yeah, ladies!" Dakota yells to the team, putting her fist in the air.

I feel a tap on my shoulder.

I turn around to see Jess. She gives me a hug. "Good job, Marley! I want to beat up the girl who knocked you down!" she says in my ear over the music.

I pull back, laughing. "Why didn't you tell me you were coming?" I yell.

She smiles and hands me her poster. "Keep it!" she yells.

I grab it. "I'll think about it!" I reply, smiling.

"*The DJ plays my song and I feel all right!*" Dakota sings, putting her arms over Jess and me.

Jess and I give each other a "might as well" shrug. So, we start to dance and sing with her.

David's not my good luck charm…Jess is.

Chapter 11

With basketball over, it means it's time for track. I have a love-hate relationship with running, so I guess I'll see how this goes. I'd prefer not running for fun, but here we are. Basketball coaches like for us to stay in shape post-season, so track is pretty much my only option. Our last home game is still the talk of the school; it was a fun night.

The seventh hour bell rings. Power walking out of math, I see Teagan across the hall. "T! You ready?" I yell.

Teagan begins running toward me, dropping her papers on the ground 'cause, of course, it's Teagan. "Crap. Yeah, Mar, wait for me!" she yells, picking them up.

Laughing, walking toward her, I say, "T, why would I leave you?" She's so goofy but I love her.

"Well, I don't know, but just in case."

I laugh and help with her papers. "Just stuff them in your locker so we can get out there," I tell her.

"Y'all wait for me, what the heck," Dakota yells from her locker.

Oh, yeah, Dakota.

I walk over to the water fountain to grab a drink. They finish getting their things together, and we head to the field to meet for our first track practice.

"I'm doing all the fast stuff. I don't do long distance," says Dakota as we're walking outside.

Jumping over the curb, I respond, "Now, that I can agree with. I'll die if I have to run any miles."

We all laugh and make our way over.

Everyone was already standing in a big circle, so all eyes are on us when we walk up because…well, when are they not.

"Thank you for joining us on time, ladies; find a spot so we can start stretching," Coach B says, embarrassing us.

We make our way into the circle. It's a rather large circle because it's both seventh and eighth-grade girls.

While Coach B is going through the sign-up sheet, I notice Jess and her friends are across from us. I am really happy we are in a sport together; it means more time for us to hang out since we don't really hang out outside of school.

"I need a few volunteers," Coach B says as I zone out in my own world.

"We will!" Dakota yells, and I feel my heart gag into my throat.

We all know I absolutely hate all eyes on me, and now, I'm pretty sure Jess is looking directly at us, considering Dakota is yelling.

"Well, there we have it, the fashionably late girls. Are you three a package deal?" Coach B asks.

"No…not at —" I start.

"Yes! We do everything together. We are like triplets!" Dakota says, smiling like SpongeBob.

Kill me now.

Coach B motions us to go to her.

Why me, Lord?

We get up there, and I'm trying not to focus on the fact that about one hundred girls are staring at us. Coach B starts explaining what we're doing to the group. As she's doing that, I happen to look at the crowd and Jess does a small waving motion to me. I smile and shrug because Dakota, duh. She laughs and shrugs back like, "Hey, she's your friend."

"Okay, so you three will do this every day as soon as we all get here," Coach B says.

Dammit, I wasn't listening. Dammit, Jess, you distracter you.

"If you aren't counting, you're running!" Coach B yells.

I am so confused. I watch Teagan and Dakota reach down to their right foot.

"One," Dakota yells.

"Two." Everyone follows.

Oh, we're leading the stretch! Wait... every day??? Oh god.

I bend over to submit to my new role that I didn't ask for.

After stretches, Coach B separates the grades and lines us up to start sprints. There are other coaches at the end of the line with stopwatches. Time to shine, I guess.

"Where's my basketball girls?" Coach B asks.

I swear people hate us from the treatment we get. Teachers treat us like we're WNBA players.

"I want y'all in the same heat. Line it up."

We make our way to the front of the group. I pass Jess on my way up and roll my eyes jokingly at her. She laughs and gives me a "woo fist pump" as I, the queen, go to show these peasants how to run.

We know I'm all talk. My heart is pounding out of my chest. Everyone is watching us like it's the damn Olympics. We line up side by side and wait for Coach B's whistle.

Coach B makes sure we're all behind the line. She blows her whistle, and we take off. I'm sprinting like I'm being chased by Pennywise. It also feels like I'm running in slo-mo because I know Jess is watching. Dakota and I are neck and neck. Teagan is a little behind us, and Alex, my basketball teammate, is behind her.

Dakota and I are neck and neck the entire way. I am trying to beat her at this point. We both cross the finish line at pretty much the same time. Teagan and Alex follow right after.

"Ha, I beat y'all!" Dakota yells in excitement. "Teagan, where were you?!" she screams, laughing uncontrollably.

Teagan looks at her with an annoyed face.

"Dakota, everything isn't a competition. We were just running for our times. We're teammates. Good job, though, y'all," Teagan says, glaring at me.

I start smiling and shaking my head because I know how Dakota is. I don't pay her any attention.

The coaches, however, were extremely impressed with my and Dakota's speed.

"Wow. You two are going to be dangerous in the relays!" Coach Tillman says in excitement.

That made me feel cool, can't lie, but I don't have to brag about it to my friends. We make our way to the side so the rest of the girls can do their heat.

After a few more heats, Jess and her friends are up.

I've actually never seen her run before, so this is new. I'm nervous for her. I don't want the other girls to beat her.

Coach B blows her whistle, and Jess takes off. She's so fast, I'm in awe. Kicking the dirt up, she sails to the finish. She smokes 'em.

"Damn, Jess is fast!" Teagan says out loud.

I'm actually impressed. I had no idea she was crazy fast like that.

"She was just against slow girls," Dakota adds with jealousy.

Teagan and I give each other "the look."

"D, stop hating on the girl; she's fast," Teagan says, shaking her head.

I'm going to go into defense mode real quick over Jess, so I'm just going to ignore Dakota.

As we stand around chatting, Coach B finishes up with the rest of the seventh-grade girls. She starts calling names after the last group goes.

"Marley, Dakota, Jess, Teagan, Brianna, Alex, and Morgan!"

We all walk from the sidelines up to Coach B.

"All right, ladies; you guys kicked butt, so now let's put you to the test," she says, smiling and rubbing her hands together as if she's plotting a heist. "Line it up!" she yells, pointing back up at the starting point.

Jess and I look at each other like, *Oh, shit.*

We all walk up to the start like we're these badass ten-time Olympic gold champions.

Coach B begins raising her voice. "Can you ladies handle the heat? We're about to find out! Ladies, cheer them on!"

I'm revving my engine, about to run like I've never run before. This is a really dramatic moment, I promise. I *need* to beat Dakota.

"On my whistle," Coach B says, grabbing her whistle.

Giving myself a pep talk, I think, *Run, Marley, run!* Jess isn't next to me, thank God. I can run in peace.

Coach B blows her whistle, and we run like a herd of buffalo.

Dakota, Jess, and I are definitely in front of everyone else. I just focus on Coach Tillman at the finish line. It feels like a seven-thousand-yard sprint. I can tell Dakota is trying to win this like her life depends on it. I'm trying to beat Dakota so she doesn't say anything rude to Jess.

All the girls are on the sideline cheering for us. I feel like it makes me run faster. You would have thought we were at an actual track meet.

"Yeah!" Coach Tillman yells, jumping up and down as we finish; it's too close to call.

"These are our relay girls! Way to go, ladies!" he says in excitement. He runs off to Coach B to discuss the results, I'm sure.

Damn, don't give me the big head now.

I wasn't in track shape, so the sprint kicked my ass. I lean over on my knees, trying to get air into my granny lungs. Jess walks over to me.

"Hey, loser," she says, smiling, giving me a light bump.

I start laughing. "I definitely beat you by a hair."

Chuckling, she says, "Marley, it's okay that you're not as fast as me." She flexes her arms like Rosie the Riveter.

"Ha! Don't even!" I say, laughing at her being goofy.

"Okay, fine. Let's ask Coach Tillman," Jess says.

"Fine!" I reply. I start walking in his direction.

"No, No! I'm kidding," she says, pulling on my arm.

Laughing, dragging her along, I say, "Oh, no, you wanna know! Let's go!"

I know Jess beat me; she's fast as hell. But to keep her around, I'm entertaining the conversation, so I drag her over to Coach Tillman to ask him who won out of us.

"It was a close one, no doubt, but you pulled it out, Jess! You ladies are crazy fast!" Coach Tillman says, as if we literally just won gold for the USA.

Jess looks at me with a smirk. We start making our way back. "Ha!" she jokes, tugging at my shirt.

"He wasn't paying any attention," I say, rolling my eyes.

Laughing, Jess pushes me lightly. "Whatever, Marley!"

We laugh, and she walks back over to her friends. I make my way back over to Teagan and Dakota.

Coach B makes us run three laps around the field before we end practice for the day. I wasn't in shape for this, and it's hot. Once we're done, we are allowed to leave. I grab my iPod and take off for my laps. Teagan runs with me and Dakota runs with a few of the eighth-grade girls.

Teagan starts talking, but I can't make out what she's saying. I turn down my music because she clearly doesn't see I'm wearing earphones. Taking them out, I say, "Huh?"

"I said track is going to be so much fun!" she says, breathing heavily.

"I know! I can't wait for our first track meet," I respond.

"Who do you think is going to be A team relay?"

I can tell she seems concerned as if she feels like she didn't do well in the last race. Dakota didn't help.

Patting her on her shoulder, I respond, "I really don't know, but regardless, we're going to have fun."

She smiles, and we finish our laps.

We make our way over to our backpacks. As I'm getting my things together, I'm unaware Jess and her friends are walking past. Dakota isn't. "You think you're fast, huh?!" she yells.

I look up to see who she's talking to. I see Jess and her friends, and Jess is looking at Dakota, confused. "Dakota," I say sternly.

Jess looks at me with the same confused face, then looks at Dakota again and shakes her head. She keeps walking.

"What the hell was that?" I say, pissed.

"Oh my god, I was just playing with her," she responds like I'm annoying her.

"That was rude as hell, Dakota," Teagan adds.

"Teagan, rude is flirting with your best friend's boyfriend," she replies.

I don't think I've ever been this uncomfortable in my life.

"Wow. Marley and I squashed that," she says.

"Well, I'm just saying, don't tell me what's rude."

I'm honestly speechless. This is the first time Dakota has actually said something about the situation. From her reaction, maybe she wouldn't do something like that to me as I thought she would. Whoops, sorry, D.

This doesn't mean I'm mad at Teagan again; it's in the past. "Guys, chill," I say as I grab my backpack. "I gotta go."

"Mar, text me when you get home," Teagan says as I walk off.

"Okay," I respond.

I had to get the hell out of that. It was extremely awkward. I'm not mad at Teagan anymore, but I also don't like to think about what happened. Besides that, Dakota said something really rude to Jess and I'm hoping she won't be mad at me for Dakota's crap. I know she knows how Dakota is, but still, I don't need her thinking I was involved. I see her in the distance, but she is getting in the car with her friends, so I can't catch up to her to apologize. She shouldn't feel awkward or uncomfortable for being badass.

"Marley!"

I see David running across the street to me. Dear god, how does he always find me?

I don't say anything.

"You just get out of track?" he asks, wiping sweat on his shirt.

"Yep. I'm so tired."

"Me too. We practiced in the gym today," he says.

"Oh, that's weird."

"Yeah."

"So," I say, looking for Mom's car.

"Everything okay?" he asks.

I check for Mom's car one last time. I don't see it.

I look at David. "Just girl stuff; you know, drama." I don't want to tell him that I'm worried sick that Jess might be upset with me.

"I'm sorry to hear that," David says. He looks at me with such empathy that I almost dive into his arms to cry on his shoulder. But I don't because that would send him the wrong signal. I'm just frustrated is all. I just want Mom to show so

I can get out of here and text Jess. Hopefully, she won't be mad at me for what Dakota did.

Mom pulls into the parking lot. Saved! I say goodbye to David and run off before he gets the chance to hug me.

Finally, I have a chance to text Jess.

Me (5:11 p.m.): Hey. I'm sorry.

Jess (5:12 p.m.): Okay, I guess. Why did she say that?

Me (5:12 p.m.): Idk, because she's Dakota. Ignore her.

Jess (5:13 p.m.): I will. Just weird.

Well, I think I'm off the hook.

Me (5:15 p.m.): I know I'm sorry :(…. You're not even that fast.

Jess (5:16 p.m.): hahahah wowwww!

Me (5:17 p.m.): :)

Jess (5:17 p.m.): :(

Me (5:18 p.m.): Lol im kidding

Jess (5:20 p.m.): :(

Me (5:23 p.m.): I am!!

Jess (5:24 p.m.): Yeah yeah.

Me (5:27 p.m.): Lol stop. I am.

Jess (5:28 p.m.): Better be. Text you later, tennis.

Damn you, tennis.

Chapter 12

A h, track meet day. This should be a fun and interesting day. Good news is we get to skip school. We do have to meet at the school, though, to gather up for our bus ride over to the track meet. Once I get off the bus (the one that picked me up from home), I immediately go to find Teagan, and I know exactly where she is: the cafeteria eating biscuits and gravy.

Power walking to the cafe, I see Teagan. "T!" I yell excitedly.

Teagan, stuffing her face with another bite, mumbles, "Mar! You ready?" She grins, slightly showing the chewed biscuit in her mouth.

"I am, but I'm starting to get so nervous," I say, sitting down next to her.

"Me, too. That's why I'm eating," she responds.

Looking at her with a smirk, I say, "T..."

We both laugh because we know she's eating because she likes to eat. Hey, so do I. Teagan is just hilarious the way she eats.

"You see Dakota?" I ask.

"Not yet; I don't think her bus is here."

"Ahh, we gotta head to the gym soon," I say, grabbing a banana and yogurt out of my bag.

Teagan grabs her phone. "I know; I'm sending her a text."

Teagan (7:43 am) to the group text: Dakota?

As we're waiting for Dakota to respond, we finish our breakfast so we can head to the gym. As I walk to dump mine in the trash, my phone buzzes.

Dakota (7:51 am): I'm not going to be there today. I'm going out of town for basketball!

Oh, shoot! I knew Dakota was going out of town but didn't know she was going to miss the track meet. Hopefully, Teagan gets to replace her spot. Oh, by the way, I run the sprint relay races. Dakota *was* first leg, Alex is second, Jess is third, and I'm fourth. Which means Jess and I get to spend a nice amount of time together in practice working on our handoffs. It's really fun and we are pretty good at it. Now that Dakota is gone, her replacement and Alex are going to have to practice when we get there so they don't screw up.

"Mar, did you see Dakota's text?" Teagan says, running up to me.

"Yeah, I had no idea she was going to miss the track meet. I thought she was leaving tomorrow?" I reply, trying not to sound slightly excited.

Teagan's giving me a facey-face. We know what the face is, so we just smile and go to grab our backpacks.

As we are walking through the halls, we are bragging to our friends how we get to miss school. You know we all do it. We feel all cool and badass and laugh at everyone making their way to their classes to die of boredom. I don't want to get behind in math, so I go to grab the work for today so I can work on it at the meet during my downtime.

"Marley? Aren't you supposed to be winning medals for us today?" Mr. Jones asks as I walk into the room.

"Ew, Marley!" Taylor P. joked.

Laughing at Taylor P., I go over to Mr. Jones's desk. "Yes, I just wanted to grab today's work so I didn't get behind."

"Okay, let me grab that for you."

As Mr. Jones goes through some papers, I sit on top of Taylor P's desk. "Ugh, Marley! Why are you here?" she says, trying to push me off.

"You see I'm waiting on my work, crybaby," I say, laughing at her trying to push me.

She gives up trying to push me off. "Fine. Let's take a selfie."

"Ew, it's too early for that," I say, not smiling for her picture.

She throws her arm around my shoulder. "Just smile for two seconds!"

"Let me get in!" Teagan yells from across the room. She had been talking with a few of our friends.

"Hurry up, Teagan; I don't have all day," Taylor P. yells.

"No...*we* don't have all day," I respond to Taylor, considering we're the ones who are supposed to be in the gym.

We take the selfie and my phone starts to ring. It's Jess. "Um, hello. Who is this?" I answer.

"Funny, Marley. Where are you? Coach B is looking for you guys so we can leave."

Looking at the clock, I notice it's 8:05 and we were supposed to be at the gym at eight sharp. "Oh crap! Tell her we're coming! I was grabbing the math homework for today."

"Maybe. Will you grab an extra for me?" she asks.

Smiling because I can't help it, I respond, "I'll think about it."

"Don't bother showing up without mine," she jokes.

I laugh. "Okay, okay! I'm hanging up now so I don't get left!"

"Bye!" Jess snaps.

"Bye, Jess." I laugh. I hang up the phone and run over to Mr. Jones.

"Mr. Jones! Do you have the paper? We have to go like right now," I say, panicking slightly.

"Sorry, Marley; I had to make copies. Here you go and good luck today!" Mr. Jones says, handing me my homework.

"Thanks!" I grab the paper and run off.

"T! We gotta go!" I yell to Teagan, who is still taking pictures with Taylor P.

We begin running down the hall when I remember I didn't get Jess a copy of the math homework. Crap.

"T, go to the gym. I'll catch up!"

I sprint down the hall like I'm on *The Amazing Race*. I bust in Mr. Jones's class, disrupting whatever they have going on.

"Marley, will you go away?" Taylor P yells to me.

Laughing and ignoring her, I run over to Mr. Jones. "Mr. Jones, I need one more copy and I'm done, I swear!" Mr. Jones laughs and hands me another copy. "Thank you, Mr. Jones. Bye, TP!" I yell and sprint out of the classroom. She's gonna kill me the next time she sees me.

I sprint down the hall, hoping a teacher doesn't see me and stop me...which I spoke into existence.

"No running, Marley!" I hear behind me. I stop in my tracks and start power walking.

My phone starts ringing. It's Teagan. I don't answer because it would only hold me back.

I look behind me and don't see a teacher, so I sprint for the doors. Once I get outside, I can see everyone getting on the buses. I'm sweating as I make my way over to Coach B.

"Ahh, there she is. I thought I was going to lose two of my girls today," she says jokingly and pats me on the back.

Okay, maybe she's not mad. Nice.

"I'm so sorry. I was grabbing my homework and it took longer than expected," I reply nervously.

"Jess let me know. All good. Hop on."

I wipe off my sweat and make my way onto the bus. Everyone starts clapping as I board. Apparently, I'm *that* late. I start laughing because they're all dramatic.

"Marley! Back here!" Teagan yells from the back of the bus. I start making my way back there.

Jess is close to the back as well; she's sitting with Dani. There's an open seat behind them, so I signal for Teagan to sit there.

"Nice, Marley," Dani says as I'm passing them.

"Hey, not my fault, okay?" I respond, laughing.

"Whose fault is it? Casper's?" she jokes.

I laugh and slide into the seat next to the window. Teagan sits on the outside. "You get your work?" Teagan asks.

"Yeah, barely made it out alive," I say, wiping more sweat 'cause I'm a sweat-aholic.

Leaning over the seat in front of me, I continue, "*Someone* made me almost miss the bus," and I hand Jess her paper.

Jess smirks and grabs it, placing it into her bag.

"Ohh, you're the culprit, Jess! I'm shocked!" Dani says jokingly, watching Jess put her paper away.

Jess laughs. "I didn't know Marley was going to take twenty years to grab a piece of paper!"

I laugh and sit in my seat. We have about a thirty-minute ride, so I pull out my iPod to listen to music. As I'm searching for a song, my phone buzzes.

Jess (8:17 a.m.): >:-)

I start laughing because she's just as goofy as Teagan.

Me (8:17 a.m.): >:-(

Jess (8:18 a.m.): I see you made the right choice.

Me (8:18 a.m.): I risked my life for your paper

Jess (8:19 a.m.): hahahah. We can work on it together

Me (8:19 a.m.): Nope. I'm going to do it by myself.

Jess (8:20 a.m.): :(

Me (8:20 a.m.): :D

Jess (8:21 a.m.): Fine.

Me (8:22 a.m.): Ugh. You know we're going to work on it together.

Jess (8:22 a.m.): I know :)

Me (8:23 a.m.): Lol I hate you

Jess (8:23 a.m.): No you don't

I don't. At all.

"I hope I get to take Dakota's spot," Teagan says to me.

Luckily, my music isn't that loud. I swear she never cares that I have earbuds in.

Looking up from my phone, I shift my body to face her. "I hope so too. I want us to do the relay together. You and Alex will need to practice handoffs as soon as we get there."

"I'm getting nervous now," she says, fiddling with her fingers. "You think Coach B will let me?"

"I'll talk to her when we get there. I don't see why not," I reply.

Dani leans over the seat. "Dakota isn't running with you guys?"

"Oh, we're eavesdropping, I see," I say, joking with Dani.

Jess joins and leans over the seat with Dani. I look at her for a split second. I can't look too long or I'll get lost.

"She has a basketball tournament out of town," Teagan says.

"What about our relay?" Jess asks.

Grabbing a granola bar out of her bag, Teagan responds, "Marley is going to ask Coach B if I can take Dakota's place."

I stare at her unwrapping this granola bar. Teagan looks at me and starts laughing. "What?! I was thinking about it!" she says as she takes a bite.

"You aren't going to have any snacks left, and we're going to be there all day!" I say, shaking my head and laughing.

Jess and Dani are still leaned over the seat, laughing at me and Teagan.

"You guys are so funny. We should hang out at the meet," Dani says.

I make a frown face at her and Jess. "Probably not," I say in a jokingly way.

Jess glares at me as if I'd better change that answer this instant. I smile cause I can't help it.

"Shut up, Mar! Yeah, guys!" Teagan adds eagerly.

Of course, I'm kidding. All I want to do is hang out with Jess. I'm just having fun with banter is all.

We have about ten more minutes until we get to the meet. I finally start up my music and rest my head on the window. When we pull up, everyone runs off the bus like a tornado is ten feet away from us. I guess they're excited. I take my time putting my things back in my bag. Jess is waiting for me toward the front of the bus.

"You didn't want to run off of here like the world is ending?" I joke.

Jess chuckles. "I don't know what that was about. I guess everyone's excited for our first meet."

"Teagan and Dani?" I ask, walking down the stairs.

"No idea," Jess answers, looking in the distance for them.

I stop to grab my hoodie out of my bag. "Wow. It's colder than I thought."

Jess already has her jacket on. I guess my adrenaline earlier wasn't letting me feel the true temperature…

"I didn't notice," Jess says sarcastically.

"Shut up," I reply jokingly.

I put on my jacket and we walk into the stadium. We see Teagan and Dani sitting in the middle of the field like they are hosting a picnic.

"I'll catch up. I need to go talk to Coach B," I say to Jess, walking down the bleachers.

"Well, wait. Are you okay with Teagan taking Dakota's place?" I ask her, stopping in my tracks.

Jess turns around. "Oh, are you asking for my opinion now, superstar?" she answers.

Shaking my head, I reply sarcastically, "No, I changed my mind. See ya." I start walking away.

Jess grabs my arm and pulls me back. "Really, Marley?!"

"I'm kidding, Jess. C'mon." I nod to her to walk with me to Coach B.

Talking to Coach B goes smoothly. She's glad to see we took the initiative to replace Dakota for this meet. She does expect Teagan and Alex to work on handoffs like I said. We make our way over to Dani and Teagan. Teagan has already opened her Gatorade and it's half empty.

"T...Why..." I laugh as I sit down.

"I need to stay refreshed, Mar. It's a big day."

"Yes, so let's eat and drink everything before the actual meet starts," I say, shaking my head.

"You guys are just like me and Jess," Dani says, grabbing her fruit snacks out of her bag.

I give her and Jess a look. "Nahh. I don't think so. You two are weird," I say, grinning at Jess.

Jess grabs one of Dani's fruit snacks and throws it at me. It catches on my shirt, so I eat it. Everyone laughs.

I put my bag behind me and rest my head on it. The cool air is making me extremely sleepy. The meet doesn't start for another fifteen minutes, so I'd like to think I have time for a power nap. I'm absolutely loving this day. I'm hanging with Teagan and Jess and we're having a really good time.

"Hey, Marley!" I hear from a distance.

I look up to see Brandon and David walking over us. I glance at Jess. "Um, hey, guys," I say, sitting up.

"Do you guys mind if we camp out here?" David asks.

Dani inserts, "The more the merrier!" She makes room in our area.

Why me, Lord, why me.

The meet still hasn't started, so we're all chilling in the middle of the football field. I put in my earbuds to finish my not-so-relaxed time. I'm annoyed David and Brandon came over. Whatever, I guess. Anyway, I'm getting a little nervous for both the meet and spending all of this time with Jess.

"Ladies!" Coach B yells, jogging over to us.

I take out my buds and sit up. "What's going on, Coach B?" I reply.

"I'm wondering why my girls are tanning in the morning sun and not working on handoffs." She kneels, tilting her shades down.

I look over to Teagan with a *whoopsie* face and grab my spikes out of my bag. "We're on it, boss," I say, saluting Coach B.

Everyone laughs, and Coach B shakes her head, smiling, and takes off for the next group to harass.

"I should go find Alex so we can practice," Teagan says, grabbing her Snickers bar.

I laugh. "I love you, T."

"Whatever, Mar!" she replies, taking off to find Alex.

"Well, boys, it's been fun," I say sarcastically. "Shall we?" I say to Jess, handing her a baton.

Jess and I walk over to an open area of the track. We have about five minutes until the meet starts.

"Are you ready?" Jess asks, nudging me.

"Are *you* ready??" I ask, bumping her back lightly.

"I'm a little nervous," she replies.

"We got this," I say, giving her a small grin.

We walk onto the track. It starts to feel more real, so the nerves are definitely setting in now. I'm also nervous because I feel like I'm performing for Jess as well. I'm a hot mess. I begin placing my tape down for my takeoff; Jess is waiting for my go. Once I'm done, I signal to her that I'm ready. She takes off sprinting. Once her foot hits the tape, I take off. Jess smoothly hands the baton to me in my left hand and I take off about fifteen meters out since we were only practicing. The handoff felt really good, though, just like at practice.

I stop and turn around, raising the baton in the air as if we'd just won a championship. Jess is celebrating, too. I walk back over. I am slightly tired from the sprint.

Breathing a little fast, I say to Jess, "Not too bad, kid."

"I know; that was so good. Wanna do one more? We only have one minute," she says.

I hand her the baton. "Lead the way, boss."

We jog to our positions.

We go through the drill one more time and it's just as smooth as all the other times. We're a good team—what can I say? We get off the track since the first race is about to begin.

"You're going to have to practice with Teagan on the field; I think she's going to be second leg and Alex will be first," I say to Jess.

"I'll have to find her then; we're after this event," she replies.

"Luckily, they have to run three miles," I say, handing Jess the baton. "I'll be sleeping."

Jess smiles and shakes her head at me. "You don't have time to sleep, Marley."

"Hey, never underestimate me," I say, grinning.

As we walk back, we run into an old friend of mine from AAU. "Marley!" I hear from beside me in the distance.

Jess and I both look over.

Jess glances at me. I look her way and back over to the girl walking toward us. It's my old basketball teammate, Victoria.

"Oh, hey!" I say as she comes in for a hug. She hugs me tighter than expected.

"This is my friend Jess," I say, trying not to blush as she lets go.

"Hi," Jess says.

"Hi, Jess! I'm Victoria, Marley's most best friend in the world," she says, squeezing my face.

God, will you just pick me up and place me like twenty meters south? Thanks. Amen.

I look at Jess, smiling cause there's someone claiming her best friend. But to everyone's defense at this age, you have like ten best friends. Jess gives me *the look*.

Jess is for sure feeling uncomfortable. For one, she doesn't know Victoria, so it's like she's third-wheeling now. I hate that feeling and since I know what it feels like, I try to cut the conversation short.

"Hey, I'll find you later on. We have to hurry and find our friends for the four-by-one," I say.

"We're in that too!" she responds. "Friendly competition? I guarantee we kick y'all's asses, though. No offense, but y'all are a white school," she says, laughing.

"One. Our school is pretty diverse, but okay, I guess. Two. We don't have our actual team today; we're missing Dakota," I say. I'm feeling pretty uncomfortable; I mean, Jess is standing right here and that was a pretty rude comment.

"Either way, again, no offense but we aren't letting white girls beat us. See ya out there!" she says, jogging off to her friends.

I look at Jess. "I'm sorry for that."

"That was pretty rude," she replies.

"Yeah, I know. Now we have to kick their ass. Let's find those two," I say, jogging off to find Teagan and Alex. Jess follows.

"Stop cursing!" she says, jogging behind me.

We find Teagan and Alex and give them the rundown. I know they aren't as fast as Jess and me, but they still have speed up under them. If they can just keep up for the first two legs, then Jess will lay everyone out on their asses and I'll bring it home. I know Jess is pissed off, too, because of that comment Victoria made, so that should light a fire under her. The comment has Teagan and Alex hyped as well. T and Jess work on their handoffs while we wait for our heat to be called.

"Okay, guys, we're about to be up. We have something to prove now," I say to the group. "I won't lie; I'm nervous as hell, but I'm gonna run like I'm running from a dog."

Jess nudges me for saying *hell*. Teagan and Alex laugh and start stretching.

Our school gets a lot of hate because it's considered to be in the suburbs. The city schools think our school is a white school, but I think it's pretty diverse. I mean, there are for sure more white kids, but overall, it's definitely one of the most diverse schools you'll find. Those types of comments always bother me.

"Ladies, are we ready?" Coach Tillman yells, jogging up to us. "Let's get to our places so we can kick some boo-tay."

We all look at Coach Tillman and laugh.

My nerves are going crazy. Track gives me nerves worse than basketball. I have no idea why.

Jess and I take off walking in the direction of third and fourth leg. "Okay, I think I'm nervous now," I say, walking Jess to third leg.

She grabs my arm and shakes me. "No, Marley! Snap out of it. We have to beat those girls!"

"I know, I know. Just nerves. I'm gonna run as fast as I possibly can," I say, giving her a nervous smile.

"You better," she says. "Or you really will have a new bff." She throws me a death stare.

I laugh. "Stop. You know you're my bff ff for life."

"Mhm," she responds, glaring at me.

"You're gonna fight me before we run?!" I say, nudging her.

"Nope. I will after," she says.

I shake my head, smiling at her.

I drop Jess off over at the third leg area. We see Victoria's teammate, and we give each other a look.

"Kick their ass—I mean butt, Jess," I say, nodding and walking off like we're in a dramatic sports movie.

I make my way over to the fourth leg area. Victoria is there, placing down her tape. "Way to show up," she says as I walk on the track.

"Ha," I say.

"What? You're still mad at what I said?"

"I mean, it was pretty rude, and you said that like Jess wasn't standing right there," I say, placing down my tape. "But it's all good, just get ready for an ass kicking."

She laughs. "Okay, Marley. Good luck."

I look down to first leg. I can see Teagan, which means Coach B put her at first leg. Oh shit, I don't think they practiced that order. Oh well, it's too late now; we'll just see what happens, I guess! I put a thumbs-up in the air and she returns it. We do the same to Alex and she puts hers up. I turn to my side toward third leg where Jess is and give her the thumbs-up. She does it back, and of course, it makes me smile 'cause I'm a sappy ass. We are locked in to kick some ass. My nerves are going crazy. I feel extremely jittery; I actually can't wait for this race to be over.

I hear the whistle blow, which means for everyone to take their marks.

The official shoots the starting pistol.

I see Teagan take off.

I'm about to throw up.

Teagan's sprinting the curve, keeping up with the pack. She's neck and neck with Victoria's teammate as she hands the baton off to Alex.

"YES! Great handoff, ladies," I say to myself.

Alex takes off for Jess. I feel like the race is happening in slow motion.

Talking to myself again, I say, "Come on, Alex. You got it."

She falls a little behind Victoria's teammate but I'm not worried since we have a secret weapon. I take a deep breath as Alex hands the baton off to Jess. Jess sprints like hell.

"You got it, Jess." I say to myself. "C'mon, c'mon…"

Jess pulls away from everyone as she approaches me. We lock eyes and prepare for takeoff. If this weren't an important race, I would have passed out from staring at Jess for so long. She hits the tape, and I begin jogging with my left hand held out behind me. She hands me the baton and I jet down the straightaway. I'm running like there's a million dollars at stake. My classmates are all on the sidelines screaming my name as I make my way to the finish line. I sprint all the way through and then some just to make sure I didn't slow down for a second.

I can't feel my legs. I look back behind me to soak in the ass-kicking I just gave Victoria.

Teagan, Alex, and Jess run up to me, and we do a wholesome group hug.

"Yes!!" Teagan exclaims.

"We did it!" Alex says, jumping up and down.

I'm still on my knees 'cause ya girl can't breathe. "Y'all kicked ass," I say, smiling.

"That's my girls!" Coach B says, running up to us. She grabs us for a group hug. "We got so many points for that race. We will need to win the rest of the relays, too, so get some rest!" she says, grinning big. I can tell she's proud.

"Carry me," I say, being dramatic.

Everyone laughs, but I was being very serious.

Whatever. Anyway, we take off for our tent and we see Victoria on the way.

"Good job," I say, smirking, and I keep walking.

I look at the group and we all smile at each other. Alex runs off to her friends as we make our way over to our tent.

"You kicked their ass," I say, grinning at Jess.

She gives me a light push. I laugh 'cause I know exactly why she pushed me.

"T, I'm proud of you. Maybe all that Gatorade was best for you."

Teagan laughs. "I told you, Mar!"

We all laugh and go to sit down. The boys are gone, thank god.

As the day goes on, we kick more butt. We wipe out all the relays for gold medals and it feels damn good. I can't lie; I feel like an Olympic champion. The day is long and I don't care. I've been with Jess the entire day and I'm having a really good time with her, Teagan, and Dani...

The four by four is the last and most painful relay we have.

I want to quit as I hit the three-hundred-meter mark. My legs burn immensely, but when I get there, Jess is on the sideline cheering me on. She is like a dose of epinephrine. I run the last one hundred meters as if my life depends on it. It's a closer race than the other relays. I had just enough energy to pick up the speed for the last ten meters to pull out the first-place win.

I walk off the track and fall out onto the turf. My thighs hurt so bad.

Jess, Teagan, and Alex come and pounce on me in excitement. "All golds, baby!" Teagan yells. "Who can stop us?"

"Calm down, tiger, before we get our asses kicked next meet," I say, laughing at her.

"You're right. I'm freezing, so I'm going to head to my mom so we can go eat," she replies, getting off the ground.

"Okey-doke. Good job today, T," I say.

"Yes, good job!" Jess says.

"You did so good!" Alex chimes in. "I'll see you guys at school tomorrow!"

"Bye, Alex!" I say, still lying on the turf.

"Bye!" Jess tells her. She looks back down at me. "Come on," she says, trying to pull me up.

"Just leave me here to rot," I say, pretending I died.

Jess laughs. "Marley, get up! Or you will be sleeping here by yourself."

I sit up abruptly. "You'd leave me here to get eaten by wolves?" I say with a surprised look.

"Yep."

I smile and get up. "Ow!" I say, trying to stand. You'd think I was eighty years old, but seriously, that race hurt so bad.

Jess shakes her head at me and laughs. "You're so dramatic," she says, nudging me.

"I didn't want all your hard work to go to waste, so I didn't really pace myself and my nerves might have gotten the best of me, too," I say, giggling.

"I know; you took off sprinting and scared me," Jess responds. "I was like, 'Oh my gosh, Marley, slow down!'"

"Oops," I say, walking over to my bag.

Jess and I grab our things. I'm sure my mom is pissed that I've had her and my family in the stands waiting. Jess and I walk to the stands to join our families. Everyone congratulates us. I don't know about Jess, but I feel like a queen.

I head out of the gate with my family. As I get to the car, I look up to see Jess and her family walking up to the car next to ours.

"You stalking me, Jess?" I say, grinning.

"Shut up," she says, grinning, annoyed at me.

I laugh and throw my bag in the car. I turn back around. "See you tomorrow, bff." I laugh 'cause you know, earlier with Victoria.

Jess rolls her eyes. "Bye, Marley."

I get in the back seat of the car and recline the seat. What a good day.

My phone buzzes just as I close my eyes.

Jess (7:57 p.m.): >:-(

I laugh and look out the window. I smile over at her and she shakes her head.

Chapter 13

There's a school dance this Friday night, and David asked me to it. How could I say no? I have to keep up appearances. After all, we are the "school couple," as my friends insist on calling us.

Jess is going with Sam, so at least I'll know someone else there. Dakota is grounded, so she won't be going. I don't mind, though. I don't feel like hearing her comments every ten seconds about David and me. And Teagan is hoping someone will ask her, but with the dance two days away, it's not looking good.

Mom wants to take me shopping for a new dress. Did I mention that this dance is a semi-formal so a dress is mandatory? Not a long dress, but something cute and casual. David will probably wear a shirt with a tie. No sport coat is needed, so the flyer that was passed out at school says.

I'm not the biggest fan of dresses. The ones I do have are collecting dust in my closet. Both of my grandmas buy me a dress every birthday and they've yet to see me wear them. You'd think they'd stop buying them. Just the thought grosses me out. I asked Mom about stockings with garters, and when she got done laughing, she threatened to throw out Kendal's Victoria's Secret catalogs.

Speaking of which, I have to admit I like to look at them when Kendal leaves them lying around. I like to look at the pretty girls and their shapely bodies. Is that normal? I mean, I wouldn't mind looking like them.

I am so dreading this dance. I'm going to have to slow dance with David. How do I not? All eyes will be on us since the school has such a fascination with us. I can't begin to think about how depressing the night will be.

Mom takes me to the most expensive store in town; she's excited for my first dance.

"Look at this one," she says, holding up the ugliest dress I've ever seen.

"Mmm, no," I say as David sends me a text asking what color my dress is. Mom says he needs to know so he can get me a corsage. That's why I need to pick out a dress *today*.

I spot a pretty yellow dress that is very simple, an A-line dress with a boatneck and slight flare. I show it to Mom, and she agrees that it will look great with my skin tone and hair. Oh, yeah, Mom says my pigtails have to come out for the dance. She's going to straighten it. I've never worn my hair straightened around my friends. I try on the dress, and it's a perfect fit. We buy it and head to the shoe department for tan shoes.

I might like this, after all. At least, the dressing up part. I haven't worn a dress since my cousin Christina's wedding two years ago. Yeah, it's been that long.

Luckily, I've done the monthly already so no worries about unsightly stains on my yellow dress!

I might not look like a Victoria's Secret model, but I just might be excited to wear a dress around my classmates. Hoodies, sweatpants, and sneakers are my go-to clothes for school. I like to be comfortable!

I think about sending text messages to Teagan and Jess to tell them about the dress but decide to wait until they see it. If Teagan doesn't get a date, I'll have her come over to help me get ready. Jess will see it at the dance.

I text David to tell him my dress is yellow. He says he can't wait to see me in it. Ugh.

The excitement for the dance mounts as everyone at school is talking about it. I feel bad for Teagan and anyone else who doesn't have a date.

The excitement is because Principal Miller announced that we are going to have live music—a band that we will love, he said. Who it is remains a mystery, and everyone has fun guessing and spreading rumors.

"It's my brother's band," Dakota brags at the lunch table.

I doubt it is because her brother is in sixth grade. He is a good guitar player, but not good enough to be playing in public yet.

Teagan works hard at finding a date, but she's not having luck. I almost want to tell her to go with David, and I'll stay home. That might not go over well with Mom, who has put a lot of money into this dance. Did I mention that she got me a purse to go with my dress? It's tan with a few yellow flowers. It matches my shoes and dress perfectly. I'd rather go to school in my underwear than hold a purse.

I think she enjoys living vicariously through me. She was dating my dad in high school, and he refused to take her to her prom. She was a queen candidate and had no date. Worse, he told her if she went by herself or with someone else, he would break up with her, so she stayed home and had to forfeit her nomination. They were young, and Mom said Dad was the jealous type back then, like a lot of high school boys.

There's just so much to look forward to—not.

⤷

It's here! The night of the big dance.

Dateless Teagan is here helping me to get ready. David is picking me up at six, and the dance starts at seven.

Are you ready for this?

He's taking me to dinner. Yes, you read that right! Dinner. And not to a fast-food joint, but to a fancy restaurant. As soon as I told Mom, she had me review table etiquette as if I can remember what fork to use. I don't. A fork is a fork, right?

Teagan slides a headband on my head. It has a daisy on it. I oddly like it.

I take one last look in the mirror as Teagan hides my dress tag. Hey, I'm so nervous, at least I didn't put my dress on inside out.

The doorbell rings. He's here. Don't panic, Marley.

Mom answers and Teagan and I start to rush down the stairs, then I remember that I must make a grand, ladylike entrance. We slow it down, and there he is. Wow! I have to admit that he looks quite handsome.

"You look great," he says, holding out a gold box.

"You do, too," I say, taking the box.

I open it and take out the wrist corsage. I slip it on, and I think I like the way it looks.

Mom gushes and tells me how beautiful I look. I kinda wish my dad were here to see me.

David's dad is waiting for us. He's driving us to the restaurant, and we'll walk to the dance because it's only a block from there.

David says goodnight to my mom and promises her that he'll have me home early. Why does he have to be so nice?

I kiss Mom on the cheek, and we leave for the car. His dad tells me how pretty I look and we're on the way to the restaurant. We are in the backseat, so David's dad must feel like a chauffeur. I feel foolish.

We're dropped off at the restaurant. David must have made a reservation. We are taken to a table that has a nice flower arrangement in the center. A waiter bring us menus.

"You can order whatever you'd like," David says, and I smile. He sure doesn't act like an annoying twelve-year-old, like Brandon, that's for certain.

"So, David," I start, "what do you want to be someday? I mean, go to college for?"

This is the type of stuff you talk about at fancy dinners, right?

"Geology. I want to be a geologist and travel the world studying earthquakes and fault lines and volcanoes."

Oh, wow. I don't know what to say. I didn't expect an answer like *that*; he sure is smart.

"How about you?" he asks.

"I'm not sure. I haven't given it much thought."

"Really? I thought for sure you'd want to do something with math, like be a math professor at a college or something. You're so good at it."

I smile. I don't know what to say. He obviously plans for the future. I can't see beyond today.

We order and our food comes quickly. I opt for a chicken salad with iceberg lettuce and no tomatoes. David feasts on a boneless chicken thigh with a baked potato. He offers dessert, and I decline. My stomach is in enough turmoil. I don't need to add to it.

I am concerned because I am sort of enjoying David's company. I think of the number of times I wanted to call it off, and right now, I'm glad I didn't.

He makes me laugh quite a few times as we walk to the school. He doesn't try to hold my hand or anything like that.

We arrive at the school gym, and the decorations are really nice. Beautiful, as one would say. David gives our tickets to Mr. Turner, one of the many chaperones, and we walk around. I look for Jess, but I don't see her. It's crowded, so maybe she's here and I can't see her yet.

There is a band, and it's one of the most popular bands in the area. They are called Pegasus, and they are hard to book. I wonder how Principal Miller managed it. Maybe because this is the alma mater of some of the band members. Either way, it's really awesome that I get to hear them live tonight. Teagan's going to be pissed!

David loops his arm through mine, and I startle. "Come with me. I see your friend Jess and she's with Sam. Let's go say hi."

This is nice of him, leading me to my friend. "Thanks for finding Jess for me," I say. I don't know; David is being really cool tonight. This might be the first time I feel like I have a boyfriend.

"Hi, Jess. Hi, Sam," I say with a smile. "Nice dress."

She reminds me of a princess. Her dress is a cold-shoulder pale-pink shift. Her shoulders peek through just enough, and I marvel at how gorgeous it looks on her.

David catches me staring at Jess. "Earth to Marley," he says, and I blush with embarrassment.

I look at Jess, and she gives me a strange look. "What? Sorry," I say sheepishly. "Your dress is just really nice; did you buy that around here?" I hope my words save me from my gawking.

"Actually, my mom and I went shopping in New York City last year, and I got it then. This is the first chance I've had to wear it." She laughs and takes Sam's hand.

I feel awkward. Very awkward. "I think I'll get some punch. Want some, David?"

"Sure," he says, and off we go.

We reach the table with the munchies and punch. David gets me a drink. He doesn't let me do much for myself. He's very much a gentleman. He holds doors open for me, he carries my books at school, he buys me ice cream at lunch… what is wrong with me? Why can't I like him the way a girl is supposed to like a boy?

The band plays a slow song, and David takes the opportunity to ask me to dance.

I accept. After all, what else are you supposed to do at a middle school dance?

We move to the dance floor, surrounded by colored lights that float in a circular direction. David, unsure of himself, wraps his arms around my waist. I loosely reciprocate. I've never danced with a boy, so I'm not sure if I'm doing this right. I can only hope it's a short song.

I look to my left and see Jess is dancing with Sam. She looks content and more sure of herself than I am.

It's times like this that I wish I had brought my phone, but in the excitement and nervousness of the night, I may or may not have purposely left the little clutch purse with my phone inside on the counter. It looks like Jess doesn't have her phone, either. She doesn't have a purse or pockets.

The music finally stops. David and I make our way to the other side of the room. Just as I'm about to lean against the wall, Jess strolls over. "Hey, can you come outside with me for a minute?" she asks.

I look at her, perplexed. "I guess so. Why?"

"Just come on," she says playfully. "You'll find out soon enough."

Jess takes my hand and pulls me along. I look back at David and shrug.

I can't imagine what she's up to.

Final Chapter

There's a warm breeze, and it brushes across me as we walk outside. "What's up?" I ask, my insides trembling. I can't imagine what this is about.

"Let's go sit over there," Jess says, pointing to a bench about ten feet away.

Oh, this can't be good. When you're told to sit, it's never good, right?

We move to the bench and sit. "What's up?" I ask nervously.

Jess crosses her hands in her lap and stares down at them. "You know we don't keep anything from each other, right?"

"Right."

"And we can keep secrets too, right?"

Again, I say, "Right."

"I really like Sam. He's a lot of fun to be with."

I don't know where she's going with all of this, and I'm trembling as if it's twenty degrees below freezing.

"I've noticed you've been hanging with Sam more," I say. Now, I stare down at my hands. My palms are sweaty, and my heart starts racing.

Suddenly, she makes a sharp turn and looks at me. "I have to tell you something, Marley."

Geez, this sounds serious. Is she going to tell me she's pregnant? Okay, that might be dramatic of me. She wouldn't do more than kiss Sam. I'm pretty sure of it. Aren't I?

"I—" Her voice trails off. "Well, I—"

"What's going on, Jess? You're being kind of weird right now. Did I do something wrong?"

"No, no, it's nothing like that," she says.

Could have fooled me.

"I, well, you've probably noticed that I haven't been hanging around with Dani lately."

"Yeah, I did notice. Did you have a fight or something?"

"No…yes…well, let's call it a misunderstanding," Jess answers.

Okay, this is getting super weird but, it's not about me, thank god. Well, I don't think it is, at least. I don't really know where this is going.

"That sucks. What happened?"

Jess sighs and turns away from me, dropping her eyes to her lap once again. "I kissed her," she blurts.

I gulp. "What? Kissed who?" I can hear my heart pounding in my chest.

"Dani. I kissed her on the lips. Just once and it was like really fast."

"You did what?"

"I kissed Dani on the lips."

"Whoa." I don't know what else to say. Did she really just say that?

"I need to explain," she says.

"Okay."

She takes a deep breath. "We'd been hanging out a lot at my house. We were goofing around and the next thing I know, I just kind of grabbed her and kissed her quick on the lips. I didn't mean to, and well…"

Silence. I'm not sure what to say, so I wait for her to start talking.

She takes another deep breath. "Look, Marley, you've got to promise me you won't tell anybody. I'm not like that. It was a foolish thing to do," she says.

"I won't tell."

What in the absolute hell is happening right now? Jess kissing Dani?! Is it weird that I'm feeling extremely jealous right now?

"I know you won't. Anyway, Dani throws her arms around me and tells me that she loves me and wants to be my girlfriend…as in dating kind of girlfriend."

"Whoa."

I seriously don't know what else to say. This is all I can say for some reason. It's all a shock. So, is Jess dating Sam or Dani? Do I ask or do I wait for her to say something? I only know of one girl-and-girl relationship, but they're in the eighth grade. Everyone is cool about it, but it's still new and different. I think everyone is curious.

"I—"

"Yeah," I say.

"Well, I had to tell her that I want to date boys, not girls, and that I love her as a friend."

She starts to sob, and I want to comfort her, but I don't know how. I get uncomfortable when people cry.

"So, what you're saying is that Dani is attracted to girls, not boys? That's um, whoa," I say.

"Yeah. She would rather be with a girl. Please don't tell anyone. She doesn't want to be made fun of or bullied, but I had to tell you. I needed to be honest with you because that's our deal, and I really needed to tell someone. You're my best friend, Marley and I knew you'd be the person I could tell who would understand."

"Of course," I reassure her. "What happens now between you two?"

"We aren't friends anymore. I can't be around her knowing how she feels about me. It weirds me out. I mean, I'm glad that she knows who she is and what she wants. I almost envy that she does. But I can't feel comfortable around her anymore knowing that she has those kind of feelings for me. And it's not fair to her. I don't want to lead her on." Jess sighs. "I made a mistake, and I think I might have given her the wrong idea. I don't know. It was stupid of me to do."

"Damn—I mean, dang," I say, smirking. "I'm sure she understands. You two were best friends. Well, second best friends. I'm first."

Jess smiles and rolls her eyes.

"And maybe by kissing her, you helped her to see who she is. Hopefully, things will settle down and you guys will get past this awkward stage."

Jess smiles. "You always know what to say to make me feel better. Maybe you're right. Maybe it did help her in a way. I still can't believe I did that."

I smile. "I'm sure it did. I must say, I'm in shock."

"I'm not one of those homophobiacs, or whatever it is they're called. I just feel like it would be hard to be around her," Jess says softly.

"I know. I get it," I say.

Jess lets out a slight laugh. "It's not easy being almost thirteen. Do you think it will get better once we're officially teenagers?"

"Probably not," I say with a laugh as my heart rate returns to normal. "I guess I get to find out next month. I'll be sure to let you know."

"You know, when I kiss Sam, I get all kinds of feelings. Like butterflies," she says.

"Oh, you kissed Sam?" I ask.

"Yeah; haven't you kissed David?"

I want to say eww, but I need to play it cool, so I say, "Not yet, but we do hug and hold hands."

Jess is quiet again, and I'm not sure what else I should say. This is all a lot for my brain to take in. I never suspected that Dani would be crushing on Jess, or maybe I did. Come to think of it, Dani was kind of possessive when she was with Jess. It made me jealous sometimes because I feel possessive over Jess.

"Hey," I say, "I think everything will be okay, and maybe someday you and Dani can be friends again."

"I doubt we will. She's pretty upset with me. I guess I led her on or something—well, I mean, I did kiss *her*, but I would never do anything like that on purpose," she says. "I mean, I never thought of dating a girl, but for some reason, she thought I wanted to date her because of it. I really shouldn't have done it. I wasn't thinking."

"Jess, don't beat yourself up. Give it a few weeks and you two will be good as new."

She turns to me with a strange look. "Hey, I forgot to tell you something else," she says.

Oh, boy. What could this be? I can't handle anything else.

She frowns. "Sam told me that the other day Teagan asked him to be her date for tonight."

"What?"

"You heard me."

"I don't know what to say. I'm not sure why Teagan would do that knowing you're dating Sam."

"I think in a way she's been jealous of our friendship; you know, since I'm your real bff." She winks. "I thought me and her were friends since we've gotten closer in track."

"Well, Teagan is, um…she doesn't think," I say, making a mental note to ask Teagan about her asking Sam to bring her here.

"I think you're right. Well, we should probably get back to our dates. They're probably wondering where we are," she says.

She stands and I stand. She faces me, takes my hands, and kisses me on the cheek near my ear. I feel the heat from her breath, and it goes through me like electricity. She hugs me, and the warmth of her body ignites mine. I think my lungs collapse because I'm having trouble breathing.

"Thank you, Marley," she says as she unlocks her embrace. "I love you like a best friend, and I know I'll never have to worry about you wanting to date me." She nudges me and laughs. "Nothing like that will ever ruin our friendship."

She starts to walk inside and stops at the door. "You coming?" she says.

"In a minute. Go ahead; I'll be right in."

She leaves, and I sit back down. What in the hell just happened? My eyes become misty. My brain is spinning around at a hundred miles an hour. I can't breathe.

I hate that she kissed Dani. I hate even more that she kissed Sam. Why? Why does it bother me so much?

I think I know why...

I stand and head back inside. I need to find David.

There's something I need to do...

CPSIA information can be obtained
at www.ICGtesting.com
Printed in the USA
LVHW091034100221
678923LV00004B/18